Does Champion have what it takes to win the Triple Crown?

Cindy sat down in the stands and looked out at the track. Champion jumped across the track a little and repeatedly asked for rein, but he seemed to be doing mostly what Ashleigh wanted.

"I hope Champion doesn't act up," Mike said, running his hands through his blond hair. "In some ways he's the biggest long shot Whitebrook's ever entered in the Kentucky Derby."

"They said that about Wonder, too," Ian said. "I remember the story well. But look how that Derby turned out."

"That's true," Mike agreed.

Cindy shot her dad a grateful look, then turned her attention to the track. Champion had just loaded in the one hole. He seemed to be waiting patiently for the other horses to join him. Ashleigh was rubbing his neck.

The other horses loaded easily. Cindy took a deep breath as the fourteen horse, the last horse in the field, was guided into the gate. *This is it*, she thought.

THOROUGHBRED

WONDER'S CHAMPION

CREATED BY
JOANNA CAMPBELL

WRITTEN BY
KAREN BENTLEY

Withdrawn

HarperPaperbacks
A Division of HarperCollins*Publishers*

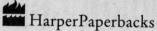 HarperPaperbacks

A Division of HarperCollins*Publishers*
10 East 53rd Street, New York, N.Y. 10022-5299

This is a work of fiction. The characters, incidents, and
dialogues are products of the author's imagination and are not to
be construed as real. Any resemblance to actual events or
persons, living or dead, is entirely coincidental.

Copyright © 1997 by Daniel Weiss Associates, Inc. and
Joanna Campbell

ISBN 0-06-106491-2

HarperCollins®, 📖®, and HarperPaperbacks™
are trademarks of HarperCollins*Publishers* Inc.

Cover art: © 1997 Daniel Weiss Associates, Inc.

First printing: July 1997

Printed in the United States of America

Visit HarperPaperbacks on the World Wide Web at
http://www.harpercollins.com/paperbacks

❖ 10 9 8 7 6 5 4 3 2

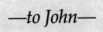

—to John—

1

"HERE, GLORY!" CINDY MCLEAN SMILED AS SHE LEANED over the top board of the paddock fence at Whitebrook, the Thoroughbred training and breeding farm where she lived. The paddocks all around her were crowded with highly bred, gorgeous Thoroughbred stallions, mares, weanlings, and horses in training. On this cold day at the end of December they had been put out to graze in the short warmth of the afternoon winter sun.

But right now Cindy had eyes only for the exquisite stallion, March to Glory. Glory threw up his head and whinnied. He galloped swiftly over to Cindy, his hoofbeats staccato and even on the frozen ground.

"You still look perfect to me," Cindy said, reaching to push the stallion's unruly forelock out of his eyes.

Glory's smooth gray coat was the color of the low winter clouds, and his sharply defined muscles bunched as he arched his neck. "I'll bet you could run as fast as you ever did," she continued. "But now you've got something just as important to do as racing, or at least you will soon."

Glory's first foal, the first foal of the season, was expected shortly on the farm. *I wonder what Glory's baby will be like?* Cindy thought as she scratched the big horse's ears. *If the foal is anything like Glory, it will really be something!*

Until a recent tendon injury had cut short Glory's racing career, the gray colt had overpowered every other horse on the track, winning the Breeders' Cup Classic and setting records in three of his races. Cindy had been Glory's exercise rider and had picked up a lot of training tips from Ashleigh Griffen, Glory's jockey and co-owner of Whitebrook with her husband, Mike Reese. Glory's thrilling victories had stunned the racing world.

Cindy jumped at a sharp snort behind her. In a nearby paddock she saw a big chestnut colt, so dark that he was almost black. Wonder's Champion had the trademark four white stockings and snip on his nose of Ashleigh's Wonder, his dam and Ashleigh's former champion race mare.

Champion's breath was white in the cold air as he huffed out snorts. He was watching her jealously. "Oh, I'll come see you in a second," Cindy reassured the colt. "Take it easy."

2

Champion lifted on his hind legs a little and shook his head. *He's not going to take it easy,* Cindy thought wryly. That had never been Champion's way.

She walked to his paddock, her riding boots crunching on the cold, hard ground. *He certainly deserves attention after his brilliant performance on the track this year,* she decided. Champion had won three out of the four races in the prestigious Kentucky Thoroughbred Development Fund Bonus Series for two-year-olds. As Champion's exercise rider, Cindy knew how lucky she was to go from one superhorse to another.

The big colt was waiting for her at the fence, his almost black eyes eager. "You are so beautiful," Cindy murmured. Champion had filled out and grown this winter. He was sixteen hands tall, and his satin coat was smooth mahogany in the pale winter light. The exquisite Thoroughbred looked every inch the champion that his name implied.

"What's the matter, boy?" Cindy asked. She climbed up the boards of the fence and nimbly jumped over the top to join the colt in his paddock. "Are you just lonesome for me?"

Champion tucked his head under her arm with a sigh. Cindy could feel her heart melting. She had never had a horse be so completely hers, not even Glory. Champion had very definite preferences in people. Almost from the day he was born, he had chosen Cindy as his favorite friend.

"In just a day you'll be three," she told the colt,

rubbing his blaze. All Thoroughbreds officially turned a year older on January 1. "I bet this will be your best year at the track ever."

Cindy had been disappointed when Champion wasn't named two-year-old champion the previous year. Sky Dancer, a colt Champion had raced against in the Kentucky Cup Juvenile Stakes at Turfway Park, had finished the year strongly with a victory in the Breeders' Cup Juvenile and won the honor.

Champion restlessly bumped her hands. "You need something to do," Cindy said. "But don't worry, boy. You'll be back in training soon." Cindy knew that Mike Reese and her dad, Ian McLean, who was head trainer at Whitebrook, planned to race Champion in the Fountain of Youth Stakes at Gulfstream on February 24.

Then Champion will be on the Triple Crown trail! Cindy's heart beat faster just at the thought of Champion running in the three races of the Triple Crown: the Kentucky Derby, the Preakness Stakes, and the Belmont Stakes. Wonder had won the Kentucky Derby and the Belmont, and her first son, Wonder's Pride, had won the Derby and the Preakness. But Whitebrook had never had a Triple Crown champion.

"Are you going to win the Triple Crown this year?" Cindy asked the colt. "Do you know how wonderful that would be? Nobody's won it for thirty years."

Champion carelessly rubbed his ear against her arm, as if to say that he wasn't worried about his chances. Cindy laughed, touching her cheek to his warm, soft neck.

"Cindy, aren't you about frozen?" called Beth McLean, Cindy's adoptive mother. She stood in the doorway of the McLeans' cottage.

"Yes!" Suddenly Cindy realized how cold she was. The gray clouds were darkening, and the scant warmth of the day was fast fading. She had forgotten to bring mittens, and now her fingers would hardly move.

Soon it would be time to bring in the horses for the night. But first, Cindy thought, she should probably help her parents get ready for the New Year's Eve party they were having that night.

Cindy walked slowly toward her family's cottage. She really didn't want to leave the horses yet. School was out for the Christmas holidays, but Cindy had spent part of the day shopping for party supplies with Beth. That had taken up a big chunk of Cindy's day. Whitebrook had over fifty horses now, and she'd barely had time to talk to all her favorite horses.

In the mares' paddock at the front of the farm Cindy saw Heavenly Choir, the mother-to-be of Glory's first foal. To her surprise, the heavily pregnant gray mare was walking up and down the fence line. For several weeks now Heavenly Choir had barely moved. With the increased weight from her pregnancy, she preferred just to stand.

Cindy frowned. She knew that sometimes mares

5

paced when they were about to foal. But Heavenly Choir wasn't due for another month. "What's the matter, girl?" she asked.

Heavenly Choir stopped at the gate and looked at Cindy expectantly. "I bet you're just hungry," Cindy said. "I'll be back soon to take you up to the barn for dinner."

As she walked along the path to the cottage Cindy saw that it was starting to snow. Giant, heavy flakes dusted her eyelashes and burned briefly on her cheeks. *Snow will be great for the holiday mood at the party,* she thought cheerfully.

For the next several hours Cindy and Samantha, Cindy's twenty-one-year-old sister, helped Beth ready the house for company. Cindy polished the furniture and cut up vegetables for dip, Samantha buffed the floors, and Beth prepared a steaming, delicious-smelling meat casserole.

Cindy heard a knock on the door. "I'll get it!" she said, wiping off her hands on a towel.

Max Smith, Heather Gilbert, and Mandy Jarvis, Cindy's best friends, stood at the door. Heather and Mandy held sleeping bags since they would be spending the night. "Hi, you guys," Cindy said. "Thanks for coming."

"The place looks great," Heather said as she stepped inside the door. Heather had been Cindy's first friend when Cindy moved to Whitebrook, and they were both horse crazy. Like Cindy, Heather rode whenever possible, although Heather didn't have her own horse. The girls were in ninth grade together. Heather was also a wonderful artist. "Wow, did you spend all afternoon getting ready for the party?" she added.

"Kind of—I'm glad it looks good," Cindy said. She was pleased with the clean, gleaming house and sumptuous buffet that greeted the McLeans' guests. "Where's your mom, Max?" she asked. "Is she on an emergency call?" Dr. Smith, Whitebrook's vet, had also been invited to the party. Max, who was also in ninth grade, dreamed of becoming a vet someday.

"No, she's here—I think we just outran her," Mandy said ruefully. "She drove us over, but I was in a hurry to get to the door."

"You're always in such a hurry, Mandy," Heather teased.

Mandy tossed her dark curls. "It's nice that I *can* hurry," she remarked. Ten-year-old Mandy was a star now on the junior show-jumping circuit, but five years earlier she had been severely injured in a car accident. She had only been walking without leg braces for two years.

"You are lucky," Heather admitted.

Mandy looked over her shoulder. "Here come Ashleigh and Mike and Christina."

"Happy New Year!" Ashleigh said, walking briskly up the path. She carried Christina, her daughter, who had just turned two on Christmas Day. Christina had her mother's sparkling hazel eyes and her father's blond hair. She loved playing with red-haired Kevin McLean, Cindy's little brother, who would turn two in May.

"Same to you." Cindy shivered as a snowy gust of wind almost banged the door shut. "Let's go inside!"

Soon the house was bustling with laughter, talk, and the clatter of plates and silverware. Len, the long-time stable manager at Whitebrook, and Vic Teleski and Phillip Marshall, both full-time grooms and exercise riders, joined the party, stamping snow from their boots as they stepped inside. "What a blizzard!" Len remarked.

"It's cozy inside." Beth picked up Kevin and set him next to Christina on the floor.

Cindy walked to the window and pushed aside the curtain. The snow was drifting softly down, blurring the yellow light from the barns. "At least snow doesn't usually stay long on the ground in Kentucky," she said. "I wanted to exercise Champion tomorrow and start getting him ready for the Florida races."

"Is getting Champion ready for the races your New Year's resolution?" Samantha asked with a smile. Red-haired Samantha was a senior at the University of Kentucky. After she graduated, she planned to work full-time at Whitebrook as a trainer and exercise rider.

"Kind of," Cindy replied, dropping the curtain. "I've got to start getting him ready for the Triple Crown."

Ian looked over from the buffet table and smiled. "We certainly have high hopes for Champion in the coming year."

"We all should be thinking about what our work for this year should be." Ashleigh's hazel eyes were thoughtful. "This should be a good year for Whitebrook. But there will be a lot of changes."

"We've got a new stallion, for one thing," Mike said, putting his arm around Ashleigh's shoulders.

Cindy knew he was talking about Mr. Wonderful, Wonder's second son. Once the brightest star in Whitebrook's racing stable, Mr. Wonderful had contracted a mysterious virus and lost the Hollywood Gold Cup and Pacific Classic the previous year. The beautiful colt had recovered from the virus, but Ashleigh had made the decision to retire him to stud at age four.

"If Mr. Wonderful can do half as well as Wonder at passing on the traits of speed, stamina, and courage, he'll be a great success at stud," Ashleigh said. "But I don't want to add too many more stallions to our roster. We really don't want Whitebrook to get much bigger than it is. I like to think of it as a small, quality operation."

Len rose from his chair. "I'm going to head down to the barns and check on the horses," he said. "I'll send up Mark."

Cindy knew that Mark Collier, Whitebrook's other full-time groom, was in the barns, keeping an eye on the horses.

"I'll come with you." Dr. Smith stood. "I want to take a look at Heavenly Choir."

"We'll be down soon, too, Len," Ashleigh said. She turned to Cindy. "We do have a big year coming up, and not just the Triple Crown or Glory's first foals. Honor Bright, Fleet Street, and Lucky Chance are now officially yearlings. They'll be broken to saddle this year."

Cindy sat in a chair close to Ashleigh to catch any news of Honor. The flashy bay daughter of Townsend Princess and Wonder's granddaughter was considered the filly of her crop to watch at Whitebrook. Cindy could hardly wait to see what the feisty filly would do on the training track.

I think Fleet Street is Ashleigh's favorite yearling, Cindy thought. Fleet Street was the daughter of Fleet Goddess, Ashleigh's other renowned race mare. Lucky Chance was the daughter of Shining, Samantha's beloved mare who was half-sister to Wonder.

Ashleigh nodded at Cindy and Samantha. "There's three of us and three fillies," she said. "That's one filly for each of us to ride this summer when we break them to saddle."

Cindy was stunned. "You're really going to let me ride one of them?" she asked, a broad grin spreading over her face. Cindy had just assumed that Ashleigh and Samantha would ride all those very special fillies.

"Sure," Ashleigh replied, smiling. "Do I have a taker?"

"You bet!" Cindy wondered which filly she would get to ride. *I'd love to ride Honor, but maybe Ashleigh wants to ride her.* Cindy knew that Ashleigh would also take into consideration each young horse's needs when she assigned riders. Cindy would be matched with the filly that suited her best.

She settled back in her chair and smiled, feeling a little dazed. *No matter which filly I get, the new year is starting off really well!* she thought.

Samantha lifted her champagne glass. "It's almost midnight—let's count down to New Year's!"

Cindy raised her glass, filled with sparkling cider, and counted with her family and friends. "Ten . . . nine . . . eight . . ."

Christina toddled over to Ashleigh and looked up into her face. "Aren't you the life of the party?" Ashleigh said with a laugh. "I think it's about five hours past your bedtime. Count with me. Three . . . two . . . one . . ." Christina struggled to count with her mother.

"Happy New Year's, everybody!" Cindy said. Cindy, Max, and Heather clinked glasses. "Hey, Mandy's asleep," Max said. The younger girl was sound asleep in an armchair, her black curls spilling over her face.

"Mandy rode for hours today, and she's probably worn out," said Tor Nelson, Samantha's longtime boyfriend. Tor had arrived late at the party after he'd finished caring for the horses in the jumping stable that he co-owned with his father in Lexington. Tor was Mandy's jumping instructor.

Cindy stood up. She felt energized from being at the party all evening and by the good news about the

11

farm's star fillies. The new year sounded like it would be a fantastic one, and she was anxious to get started on it. "Let's go see the horses now that they're a year older," she suggested.

The cottage door burst open, letting in a swirl of wintry air. Len poked his head in the doorway. "Happy New Year," he said. "Come on down to the barn, everybody. I've got a surprise."

Cindy stared at the farm manager. Only one thing could make Len smile like that. "Heavenly Choir had her foal!" she burst out.

"You bet." Len winked. "A filly. I would have called you all to come down, but things happened fast. Dr. Smith and Mark are with them now."

"This is so great—I can't wait to see them!" Cindy grabbed her coat and rushed to the door. Max, Heather, and Mandy hurried after her.

"Len, is the foal all right?" Ashleigh asked, sounding concerned. "She's almost a month early."

"She's up and nursing," Len assured her.

The night was frosty and still as Cindy pushed through the deep snowfall. The stormclouds had cleared, and a low moon hung on the horizon, its white light reflecting off the smooth, untouched fields of snow. Cindy shivered with cold and anticipation. *I just know Glory's colt will be as beautiful and perfect as this night,* she thought.

The mares' barn was hushed and peaceful, lit only by night-lights. Toward the far end of the barn Cindy saw brighter light coming from Heavenly Choir's stall.

Inside, the big gray mare stood quietly, her head low. On the far side of her Cindy saw only the flick of a short tail. Dr. Smith was just stepping out of the stall.

"Can I go in?" Cindy asked eagerly.

"Sure. You know what to do." Dr. Smith smiled.

Quietly Cindy unlatched the stall door and walked to Heavenly Choir. "Hi, girl. It's just me."

The mare whoofed tiredly, then turned her head to sniff her foal. Cindy's heart was thumping with anticipation as she looked around Heavenly Choir to get her first glimpse of Glory's foal.

The almost black baby was standing precariously on her long, slender legs. Her short, fuzzy mane and tail were almost black, too. She stared at Cindy, her big eyes luminous in the dim light.

"Come here," Cindy whispered, almost overcome with joy. "Let's get a good look at you." The foal took a few stiff steps toward her. Then she wobbled and almost fell.

"That's it," Cindy encouraged. "Aren't you a pretty one?"

Encouraged by her voice, the foal stepped trustingly over to her. Arching her lovely dark neck, she sniffed Cindy's fingers.

"She looks just like Glory," Cindy exclaimed, running her hand gently down the foal's shoulder. She glanced back at Dr. Smith, her family, and her friends. "Glory's first foal is just like him!" she added.

"Yes, she is," Dr. Smith agreed. "She's a little small, but perfectly healthy as far as I can tell."

"She couldn't be more gorgeous." Cindy knelt beside the foal to give her a soft hug.

"No one's going to disagree with that." Ashleigh was beaming.

"She's so black!" Mandy observed, leaning over the stall door.

"Her muzzle is lighter, though," said Dr. Smith. "She's going to be a gray. Gray horses are born dark and lighten with age."

Cindy rocked back on her heels and studied the foal. "You were born on the first day of the new year," she said. The small foal watched her intently. "I think you're going to be first in everything for your whole life!"

"We're so lucky she didn't come a day earlier," Samantha said. "Then she would have been a year old today, at least officially."

Suddenly the foal's spindly legs went out from under her and she plopped into the straw. "You're tired, aren't you?" Cindy said gently. "It's been a big day."

She sat down in the straw, gently cradling the tiny foal's head in her lap. The stall was warm and quiet as the foal slept. Heavenly Choir was dozing.

Cindy's heart overflowed with love, pride, and happiness. The Christmas spirit, and all the hope of a new year and a new life, seemed to linger in the stall.

Cindy touched her cheek to the foal's soft coat and closed her eyes. *I don't have to think very hard about a name for you,* she thought. *You're going to be Glory's Joy—and mine, too.*

2

"SLOW TROT, CINDY," ASHLEIGH CALLED THE NEXT MORN-
ing as Cindy walked Champion through the gap to
Whitebrook's mile-long training track. "Take him
once around."

"Got it." Cindy gathered Champion's reins and
looked ahead to the first curve in the track. The
track's surface glistened with ice crystals, and the
mist from the melting snow hung like a heavy breath
over the rolling hills.

Cindy smiled, enjoying the clean smell of wet, melting snow. *I'm just glad the snow didn't stay on the ground
so I could get out here with Champion*, she thought. Cindy
was beginning the colt's warm-ups to put him back in
training for the Fountain of Youth race in six weeks.
Then, following the classic trail to the Kentucky Derby,
Champion would run in the Florida Derby.

Cindy shifted her weight slightly forward in the saddle, asking for a trot. Champion sprang ahead instantly, his movements light and floating. The big colt glanced back at her and tossed his head. His look was affectionate but a little mischievous, too. Champion yanked suddenly on the reins and gave a little hop.

"I know you feel good, but behave yourself, Champion," Cindy warned. She could easily sit out a little hop like that, but the colt was capable of much worse behavior. Champion had won most of his races the year before through sheer talent, but sometimes just barely. He had lunged at the crowd in the walking ring, reared in the gate, and chased other horses on the track.

That was partly my fault, Cindy thought. After the death the previous spring of Storm's Ransom, Whitebrook's brilliant gray sprinter, Cindy had trouble putting her heart into Champion's training. But in the difficult months following Storm's death, Wonder's beautiful colt had come to take more than Cindy's time and attention. Through her love for Champion, Cindy had finally put her grief over Storm behind her.

The fresh cold stung her cheeks as Champion trotted on, shaking his head. Cindy pushed her blond ponytail over her shoulder and settled deep into the saddle. "I've probably ridden you a hundred times, but I'll never get over how smooth your trot is," she murmured.

Champion's ears flicked back at her voice. Cindy

smiled, reaching to rub the colt's sleek shoulder. In no time they had circled the track.

"What now?" Cindy called to Ashleigh. Cindy saw her dad and Mike walking up the path to the gap, followed by Samantha, riding Limitless Time. The bay three-year-old son of Fleet Goddess had raced once as a two-year-old but come in second to last. Cindy knew that her dad, the colt's trainer, hoped Limitless Time had grown up and would do better in his three-year-old season.

"Let's just keep Champion at a trot today," Ashleigh said, looking closely at the colt. "Take him a couple of times around and let him get used to the track again—and to you."

Champion was gazing at the track, his eyes bright and interested. "Okay, Champion," Cindy said. "Let's try a circle right here first." At the touch of a rein Champion did a tight circle easily, until he was facing the gap again.

Cindy nodded with satisfaction.

"Good," Ashleigh said. "He hasn't forgotten his training."

"I didn't really think he would." *Champion's one of the smartest horses I've ever known*, Cindy thought. That had been part of the problem in training him. The colt never forgot anything he learned, whether good or bad.

Cindy asked Champion for a trot again, and the colt snorted as he jumped ahead. He seemed to be saying, Let's go!

"Sorry, boy," Cindy said with a laugh. "Ashleigh wants us to do a slow trot—*not* a dead run."

Cindy glanced over her shoulder at the sound of quick snorts behind them. Silken Maiden, a bay four-year-old filly, was coming up on the inside of the track, with Mark riding. Bought at the Keeneland select yearling sale, Silken Maiden had a golden pedigree, with three champions in her immediate pedigree. The filly had been plagued by injuries and had just returned to training.

"Hey, Cindy!" Mark raised a hand briefly.

"Good morning, Mark." Champion skittered a little sideways, and Cindy swiftly recalled her thoughts to her own mount. Champion could be a handful, especially when other horses were around. Automatically Cindy tightened her reins. Then she reminded herself not to anticipate trouble with Champion. The colt reacted badly to not being trusted.

To Cindy's relief, Champion let the bay filly pass with hardly a flick of his ears. "That's a boy," she praised, stroking Champion's dark brown neck. "You don't need to bother with her right now because we're not running. We're just warming up, and you seem to know that. Maybe this year you won't go after other horses."

Cindy knew Champion would have to keep his mind on his work. With the Triple Crown races coming up, he would need every ounce of talent and courage he possessed to take on the best horses in the world.

19

"I wonder how you'll do as a three-year-old," Cindy said to the colt. The colt was huffing clouds of breath into the gray morning air and prancing, his feet lightly sucking in the wet dirt. "You've got Wonder's heart, and you're sweet and affectionate like she is—at least around people you like. But you've got a fiery side, like your sire, Townsend Victor. I think you've got both of your parents' talent, though."

Champion eyed her backward, his hooves steadily churning the soft track. Cindy was glad that the colt seemed to be handling the muddy surface well. Of course, they were only going at a trot. The previous year Champion had lost the Kentucky Cup Juvenile Stakes on a muddy track. But the track condition might not have been the only reason he lost. Secret Sign, a horse Champion hated, had also been in that race and had distracted him.

"Are you going to go after other horses this year?" Cindy asked Champion, looking across the track. Vic and Freedom's Ring, a black three-year-old colt, were just crossing the gap. "We're going to try something," she murmured, gathering her reins. For some reason Champion had never liked Vic or Freedom. Cindy wanted to see what Champion would do if she rode near them.

Ashleigh was giving Vic instructions at the gap. Cindy thought Champion's ears went back a fraction as he approached Freedom, but she hoped she was just imagining it. "Hi, Vic," she said. "Would it be okay if I rode beside you for a few minutes?"

Vic grimaced. "I don't know, Cindy. Champion just doesn't like me. Why push it?"

"Because you're not the only person he doesn't like," Ashleigh said. "More important, Champion doesn't like Freedom. Let's see if Champion will behave this morning going slowly with you two, Vic. If he doesn't, we'll have to figure out a way to get him over it."

"All right." Vic didn't sound happy.

Cindy looked at Champion as they set off at a walk, with Champion on the inside. The colt was keeping his distance from Freedom, and his ears were pricked. *So far, so good*, she thought.

"Let's pick it up to a trot," Vic suggested. Before Cindy could reply, he put Freedom into the faster pace.

Champion's ears swept back. "Look out!" Cindy cried. In an instant she saw that Champion wasn't going to let go of it there. The colt bore out sharply, trying to shoulder by Freedom. *He wants to get ahead of Freedom, but this isn't how to do it!* she thought desperately.

Cindy pulled Champion's head hard to the inside and applied pressure with her outside leg. The sensitive colt moved over just enough to avoid bumping Freedom. But his mouth was open, and he was trying to bite Vic. The colt's jaws closed on air.

Cindy urged Champion forward at a fast trot, pulling away from Freedom. "Champion, that was terrible," she scolded. "What gets into you?"

The unrepentant colt tossed his silky mane and

21

trotted on. He seemed pleased that they were in front of Freedom now. Vic was holding the black colt at a safe distance back.

"That was close," Vic called.

"Champion sure didn't want you in front of him." Cindy shook her head.

She looked back at the gap. Ashleigh was standing very still and seemed to be thinking hard. Cindy was certain that she knew what Ashleigh was thinking about.

We've still got a problem with Champion, she said to herself as the colt's quick strides rapidly took them around the track. *This year I've really got to solve it, or he won't be running in the Triple Crown races. He could get hurt—or even killed.*

"I feel like I'm at a movie theater," Heather said that afternoon as she reached for the popcorn bowl in Cindy's living room. Cindy had invited her friend over to Whitebrook to watch videos on the big-screen TV of Townsend Victor, Champion's sire, in his races. Cindy and Heather had just finished watching Wonder win the Kentucky Derby.

"It's better than that—they hardly ever show movies of famous racehorses at the Cineplex." Cindy propped her feet on a footstool and studied the video intently. Townsend Victor was running in the Jim Beam, a Triple Crown prep race. Cindy had watched the video before, and she knew this was Townsend Victor's last race.

Cindy leaned forward in her chair, drinking in the magnificent colt's effortless running style as he swept around the far turn for home. She could almost feel Townsend Victor's pleasure in speed as he reached for ground, six lengths ahead of the rest of the field.

"He's a beautiful horse," Heather said. "He looks just like Champion."

"He does. He's the same color and build." Cindy frowned. "Townsend Victor runs like Champion, too. That's why I'm watching this."

"He has a superdrive like Champion's, doesn't he?" Heather asked.

"I think so—I'm trying to see." Cindy cupped her face in her hand, then pointed at the screen. "Look at this. Here comes Pacesetter up on the outside to challenge, crowding Victor a little. . . . There!" Cindy stopped the video. "That's right where Victor went into his superdrive."

Cindy narrowed her eyes as she examined the lovely colt's action in midstride.

"He's reaching so high, he almost looks like he's jumping," Heather said.

"Yeah. But I don't think he really has another gait," Cindy said. "It's just an amazing closing kick. When Victor and Champion are challenged, they put out a big burst of speed."

"They sure do," Heather said. "Victor's really flying." Cindy looked at the frozen video for another second, her hand hovering over the remote. Townsend

Victor had been so strong and full of life. Cindy could hardly stand to start the tape again. She knew that in a stride or two, Townsend Victor would break down and never run again.

Just do it, she ordered herself, picking up the remote. *You have to understand what happened.*

Cindy pressed play. "Now watch. Victor doesn't keep up his superdrive."

The girls watched as Townsend Victor jerked his head to look at the other horse and dropped off the pace. Victor's jockey started to pull the colt's head around, but it was too late.

Townsend Victor bore out sharply, charging at the other colt. But before Victor could reach him, he slowed dramatically. In an instant he had dropped back behind Pacesetter, limping badly on his right forefoot. Cindy could see the jockey trying to pull him up quickly, but Victor fought him at every step. The jockey finally stopped him just after the wire.

Cindy sighed heavily. *That happened so fast*, she thought.

Both girls were silent for several moments. "How did Victor get hurt?" Heather finally asked. "It didn't even look like he hit the rail."

"He didn't. He just got off stride and put too much pressure and weight on his right front leg." Cindy stopped the video and began to rewind it.

"Do you think that was the jockey's fault?" Heather asked.

"Not really." Cindy tipped back in her chair and frowned. "Victor went out of control so fast. Maybe the jockey should have expected trouble with Victor when the other horse went by."

"That was hard to watch." Heather looked at her fingernails.

"Yeah, it really was," Cindy agreed. Every time she saw the video of Victor's last race, she felt sick and scared. "And I've watched it a bunch of times. But Champion runs so much like his sire, and his personality is a lot like his, too. I have to be sure we don't make the same mistakes with him."

"But Champion's always been treated well. Didn't you say that a jockey mistreated Victor until he got kind of crazy?" Heather asked.

Cindy nodded. "Victor was a Townsend Acres horse, and the Townsends let Victor's first jockey whip him. Victor probably hated people after that. This time when I watched the video of the Jim Beam, I even kind of thought Victor was going after the other jockey, not Pacesetter."

"Victor sure wasn't listening to his own jockey," Heather said.

"No, and that's bad. That's why the accident happened." Cindy stood and stretched. "Let's go see Champion now and give him a lot of love." She wanted to get out of the house and away from those bad memories.

"You give Champion a lot of love every day." Heather smiled.

"Yeah, but today I have a special reason." Cindy's mouth still felt dry after that awful video. "I want to make sure Champion knows there are people in the world he can trust. I don't want Champion's career to end the way Townsend Victor's did."

3

"HEY, CINDY!" LAURA BILLINGS HURRIED DOWN THE HALL at Henry Clay High School on the first day of school after the Christmas vacation. "Wait up."

Cindy stopped just outside her English Skills classroom to wait for Laura, waving to some other people she knew. *It's nice to feel at home*, she thought. *I really feel like a high school student now that we're starting the second semester.*

Laura stopped in front of Cindy, breathless.

"Slow down, why don't you?" Cindy asked with a laugh. Laura, also a ninth grader, was one of the most high-energy people Cindy had ever met. Cindy often ate lunch with Laura and some other friends from her class.

"I can't slow down," Laura said, pushing her dark brown bangs out of her eyes. "We've got a social planning committee meeting after school, and I have to tell about six other people before class. The meeting will just be a short one to plan the winter dance."

"I heard about the meeting from Heather." Cindy had joined the ninth-grade social planning committee the previous fall. The committee planned dances and other special events for the ninth grade. "I'll be there," she added. Sometimes Cindy had to miss meetings because she had so much to do at home with the horses.

"Okay." Laura was already walking down the hall. "Tell Max, will you?"

"Sure." Cindy had English Skills with Max the next period. Cindy was almost late for class, and she barely had time to take a seat next to Max before her new teacher, Ms. McGaughey, began calling roll.

"This isn't going to be an easy class," the teacher warned after she had called the last name. "Some of you may have coasted in your other classes, but you'll work here. I see this class as preparation for college."

Cindy raised her eyebrows and looked at Max. He shook his head.

"We'll have a quiz every Thursday and a book report due every Friday," Ms. McGaughey continued.

Cindy groaned along with the other kids. *At least college won't be hard after this!* she thought. Max rolled his eyes.

Cindy leaned across the aisle. "Social committee meeting after school," she whispered.

"Okay," Max said.

"Ms. McLean and Mr. Smith," the teacher called. "This isn't social hour."

Cindy sat back in her seat and folded her hands. All she needed was detention on top of that quiz and book report the first week. *I guess I'd better be an angel for the rest of the period*, she thought with a sigh. *Otherwise I won't see the horses until spring—I'll be sitting here until it gets dark every day.*

The ninth-grade social committee met in one of the library rooms after school. Cindy walked between the tall bookshelves toward the soft sound of her friends' voices, enjoying the smell of paper, ink, and old books.

The other committee members were already seated around a long conference table. "Hi, Cindy." Laura, the president, sat at the head of the table. "We were just trying to figure out the theme of the dance. Heather thought we should have a winter sports theme. The dance floor could be the ice skating rink. Then we could paint skiers and mountains on paper and tape it to the walls."

"Sounds neat." Cindy set her books on the table. She usually didn't have time for winter sports, but she could ice skate pretty well. The sports theme would be fun and festive, she decided.

"Let's do something different at this dance," Melissa Souter said. "What if we gave some of the proceeds to charity?"

"We could charge a dollar or two extra for admission," Max agreed.

"Or hold a raffle," Laura suggested.

Cindy held up a hand. "Wait. We have to decide what charity the money is going to."

"I have an idea about that," Heather said shyly. "My mom does volunteer work at the animal shelter. I heard they need money to expand the space so they can keep more dogs and cats."

"That's a perfect idea, Heather!" Cindy said eagerly. She couldn't think of a better cause. Like the abandoned and unwanted animals in the shelter, Cindy had been an orphan once, shuttled between bad foster homes.

"So why don't we hold the raffle at the dance?" Max asked. "What should we raffle off?"

"A lot of kids like Heather's paintings," Sharon Rodgers said. "Could you donate one of those, Heather?"

Heather blushed. "Sure," she said. "If you think people would really want one."

"Lots of people would." Cindy frowned at her friend. Heather was the best artist in the school. *Sometimes Heather's just too modest for her own good*, Cindy thought.

"Let's come up with really cool prizes," said Susan Griegos. "Not just junk out of somebody's attic."

"I'll donate a ride on a Whitebrook Thoroughbred as my raffle item," Cindy volunteered. "If the winner is an inexperienced rider, I'll put him or her on one of the gentler, older exercise horses. But if the winner has riding experience, we could go on a trail ride together."

"Great prize, Cindy." Max said. Several of the other kids nodded.

"To raise more money, why don't we sell raffle tickets to whole families?" Melissa said.

"And to the whole school, not just the ninth grade." Sharon nodded. "The winner wouldn't have to be there to get the prize."

"All right, that's decided," Laura said. "Now let's figure out the details of the dance. Heather, I hope you're going to help us decorate again."

The committee members had worked together on two other dances, and soon they had a plan of action for the dance. They voted to hold it on February 3.

"Do you want to go to the dance together?" Cindy asked Max as they pushed back their chairs to leave.

Max glanced at her sideways. "Sure, as long as you're asking me just as a friend," he joked.

"I am." Cindy smiled. She knew Max was referring to a tense time at the beginning of the school year, when he had asked her to a dance. Cindy had misunderstood, thinking he wanted to be her boyfriend. Now they had gotten that all cleared up. Sometimes they went to the movies or to events together, but only as friends.

"The dance should be fantastic," Cindy said as she walked with Max and Heather to the pay phones to call home. "Should we plan a shopping trip to look for new dresses?" she asked Heather.

31

Heather nodded. "I can't wait to see who everyone's going with," she said.

"Me either—and what everybody wins at the raffle," Cindy agreed.

Right after she got home, Cindy drove over to Tor's stable with Samantha to watch Mandy's jumping lesson. She and Samantha couldn't stay long because they had to help with the evening chores at Whitebrook. But Samantha wanted to spend at least a little time with Tor, and Cindy hadn't seen one of Mandy's lessons in weeks. She was eager to see her friend's improvement.

"It's nice of you to stop by and watch Mandy," Samantha said as she turned into the stable drive.

"I like to come watch." Cindy knew that Mandy worked incredibly hard at her riding. Mandy and Butterball, her pony, were already a great jumping team.

Samantha frowned. "I've heard that Mandy's parents *don't* like watching her these days. They think she takes too many chances."

"Maybe, sometimes." Mandy had taken a couple of bad falls, and she often wore herself out, but she won a lot of shows. "Do you think Mandy takes too many chances?" Cindy asked.

"Well, she's an excellent rider," Samantha admitted. "And I guess you and I are ones to talk about dangerous riding, since we ride racehorses! But somehow it's different for Mandy. She's been through so much in her life already."

Cindy knew that Samantha was referring to Mandy's severe injuries from the car accident when she was five. Mandy had almost completely recovered now, but Cindy could understand that her parents would hate to see her in danger.

Jumping is a dangerous sport, Cindy thought as she followed Samantha to the stable. *I guess I can't blame Mandy's parents for being worried.*

The early winter night had fallen, and the horses were all inside the barn. Cindy always liked visiting the Nelsons' stable. Several of their jumpers were Thoroughbreds, her favorite kind of horse. But the race they ran was between fences on a jump course, not on the track.

"I'm going to the ring to look for Tor," Samantha said.

"I'll be right there." Cindy wanted to look at the horses for a minute.

As she walked down the broad aisle in the brightly lit barn, Top Hat, Tor's retired champion jumper, put his head over the stall door, asking for a caress.

"You're a good old boy, aren't you?" Cindy asked, rubbing Top Hat's muzzle. With his roman nose and oversize ears Top Hat would never win a beauty contest, but he had taken first in jumping at the National Horse Show.

Cisco, a gray gelding in the stall next to Top Hat, whinnied sharply. "You must be lonesome with your owner gone so much," Cindy sympathized. Cisco belonged to Yvonne Ortez, Samantha's best friend from high school. Yvonne had ridden Cisco in the National Horse Show years earlier. Now she worked in New York City as a clothes designer and model.

Cindy gave the gelding a final pat. "See you later, guy," she said. "I'd better go watch Mandy." Cisco whinnied again.

Mandy sat quietly at the far end of the ring on Butterball, her small caramel-colored pony. A challenging course of jumps had been set up around the ring: three colorfully striped verticals and two oxers, an in-and-out, a brush jump, and a water jump. Some of the fences were almost three feet tall.

Cindy settled in the bleachers next to Samantha to watch. She knew Mandy was getting her focus to take the jumps and hadn't seen Cindy at all yet.

Mandy gave a small nod and gathered her reins. The little pony launched himself gamely at the first vertical and cleared it with ease. Mandy was already looking at the next obstacle, an in-and-out with just a stride between fences. She quickly turned Butterball after the vertical and immediately asked him for more speed to take the in-and-out.

Cindy smiled as she watched the younger girl tear at the fences. "Way to go, Mandy," she whispered to Samantha. Samantha nodded.

Butterball bounded over the first jump of the in-and-out. With just one quick stride in between he sprang over the second. Mandy's head was up, her shoulders were straight, and her heels were down. Her form over the jump looked perfect to Cindy.

The pony and girl cantered toward the next fence, a broad brush jump, and flew over it with ease. *Butterball's small, but he always gives his best,* Cindy thought.

She looked at her watch. It was almost six o'clock. That meant Mandy had been riding for an hour already. *You never would know.* Cindy wondered if Mandy got tired more easily than other people because her legs were still weak. *I bet she does, but she keeps riding anyway,* she thought.

"That's good, Mandy," Tor called when Mandy had completed the eight-jump course. "Come over here for a second."

Mandy circled Butterball. For a second Cindy wondered if Mandy was about to take the course again. Then Mandy checked the pony and posted over to Tor.

"You looked good, but you're still anticipating the jumps a little and so is Butterball," Tor said. "You're taking off early as a result, and Butterball's having to make a bigger jump and work harder. You can get away with it now, because he's an athletic jumper, but you'll take down higher fences. You don't want to make a habit of jumping higher and farther than you have to."

Mandy nodded seriously. A tall, dark-haired young woman entered the ring and looked around with a smile.

"Yvonne!" Samantha cried, jumping to her feet. "I didn't know you were going to be in town."

35

"I couldn't stay away from you and Cisco any longer," Yvonne said as she hurried to the bleachers. "Hi, Cindy—I've heard about the wonders you've worked with Champion."

"He's a great horse." Cindy had met Yvonne a couple of times when Yvonne visited Kentucky. *So Champion's fame has spread to New York City!* she thought.

Samantha and Yvonne hugged. "Tell me the news from New York!" Samantha demanded.

Yvonne sat down in the bleachers beside her friend. "I'm so busy," she admitted. "Life is really fast paced in New York! Especially in the fashion industry—it's cutthroat competitive. But I haven't given up on designing my own line of clothes someday."

"You shouldn't," Samantha said. "You have such style."

Cindy had to agree with that. Yvonne wore close-fitting designer jeans and a boxy, black velour top with black low-cut riding boots. Her hair was French-braided with bright red ribbon that set off the brilliant sheen of her black hair. Cindy knew that Yvonne was part Spanish, Navajo, and English. She had moved to Kentucky from New Mexico, and she and Samantha had gone to high school together.

"Now you tell me the news from Whitebrook," Yvonne said. Soon the two friends were deep in a discussion of the farm's horses.

Cindy slipped out of the bleachers to meet Mandy. Mandy was leading Butterball to the side of the ring, slapping her boot with her crop. "Hey, Cindy," she said. "Thanks for coming! What did you think of the lesson?"

"I think you get better all the time," Cindy said honestly. Mandy's boots and breeches were covered with dust, and she seemed to be leaning on Butterball for support, but her dark eyes shone. Butterball rubbed his small ears against Mandy's arm, and Mandy firmly gripped his shaggy mane.

"I've kind of reached a wall with Butter, though." Mandy frowned. "He's just too small for the kind of competitions I want to enter."

"Well, maybe Tor could sell him for you," Cindy said slowly. She couldn't imagine Mandy without Butterball. The younger girl had ridden him for years.

"Oh, I don't mean I'd sell Butter!" Mandy looked stricken. The pony nudged her, as if he couldn't believe it either. "I hope my parents let me keep him forever. I want to get *another* horse."

"Tor could help you with that, too," Cindy suggested. "A lot of people mention to him that they have horses for sale."

Mandy was frowning again.

"What?" Cindy asked. *It's no wonder Mandy rides jumpers*, she thought. *Her mind is always about two jumps ahead even in a conversation!*

"I want to train my own horse," Mandy said with finality.

Cindy could feel her jaw dropping. "But that would take years!"

"Maybe." Mandy shrugged. "But I have to do it. I'm going to need a top-notch horse. See, I want to do three-day eventing. For sure I want to try cross-country jumping. I think I'd like it."

"Isn't cross-country even more dangerous than show jumping?" Cindy asked. "I mean, the jumps don't fall down when you hit them in cross-country, the way they do in show jumping."

"I know, I know," Mandy said impatiently. "But I won't hit them. That's what I'm telling you—I need a really good horse to ride cross-country."

"I see." Cindy supposed Mandy did need an excellent horse to ride cross-country. But she wondered if Mandy had bitten off more than she could chew. "Did you tell your parents about riding cross-country and training your own horse?" she asked.

Mandy hesitated for the first time. "Not yet," she admitted.

I wonder what they'll say, Cindy thought. *Something tells me they won't like this much.*

4

OVER THE NEXT SEVERAL WEEKS CINDY CONTINUED TO EXER-cise Champion, slowly building up his stamina for the Fountain of Youth race in late February. The days warmed up as deep winter passed, and there was more light in the afternoons. Cindy could spend more time after school with the horses.

Every day that the snow wasn't too deep she rode Champion into the hills, building his stamina. The colt lightly stepped over rocks and branches, his muscles supple and powerful. He bounded up the slopes, tossing his head from the sheer joy of being outside.

Cindy loved the time she spent with her horse. Sometimes she rode him to the small creek that cut through Whitebrook. She would stop Champion on the bank and sit quietly for a few moments, listening to the bubbling of the fresh, cold water against the rocks and admiring Champion's beauty. The colt's sable coat was a dark splash against the snow-dusted ground, and his finely molded head was the picture of perfect Thoroughbred breeding. Cindy's heart swelled with pride every time she looked at him.

"Do you smell spring coming?" she asked Champion one Saturday as she tightened the girth on his saddle in the barn. The late January morning was still cold, and gray clouds shrouded the far hills. But Cindy thought she caught a faint whiff of spring in the damp, earthy-smelling air.

Champion shook his thick dark mane and snorted. Then he twisted his neck to look at Cindy.

"I know, you want to get going—spring means racing to you," Cindy said, ruffling the colt's mane with her hand. "I want to get out on the track, too."

Cindy led the eager colt outside the barn to a mounting block and lightly sprang into the saddle. Then she adjusted her stirrups and asked the colt for a walk.

Champion's muscles rippled and his neck bowed as he tried to be good and keep to the slow pace. The pale winter sunlight glinted off his deep brown coat.

Cindy felt a momentary pang. *He looks so great, and that means he'll be leaving soon,* she thought. In just two days Champion would be vanned to Gulfstream to begin intensive spring training.

"I'll miss you," she said softly. "But this spring is

going to be so exciting, and I'll be with you for all your big races. And guess what—today I get to let you all the way out on the track. Ashleigh wants to see how fast you are now that you've grown up some more."

Champion charged ahead at a trot for a few paces, as if he couldn't help himself. Then, with a jerk in his stride, he settled back into a walk.

"I think you know just what's coming, Champion," Cindy said with a laugh. "You always do. But you've got to listen, boy, not just go fast. You need to remember every bit of your training from now on. The Fountain of Youth isn't going to be a walk in the park. And the Kentucky Derby and other Triple Crown races sure aren't either."

Champion ignored her. His eyes were fixed ahead on the track, and his ears were pricked. The track was almost empty because most of the horses had already gone back to the barn. Ashleigh had told Cindy that she wanted to work Champion at ten, and so Cindy had luxuriated in bed until almost seven o'clock.

Ian and Len stood at the rail, watching Ashleigh trot Limitless Time back to the gap. "I'll be with you in a minute, Cindy," Ashleigh called, hopping out of the saddle. She and Ian conferred for a minute.

They must be talking about Limitless's allowance race at Gulfstream, Cindy thought. She knew that her dad, Mike, and Ashleigh hoped Limitless would be ready for a stakes race later in the spring season.

41

"I'll take Limitless back to the barn," Len volunteered.

"Thanks, Len." Ashleigh looked up at Cindy. "Are you ready to take Champion out there?"

Cindy nodded, wondering why Ashleigh would ask her that. *We're ready to get out there every morning!* she thought.

"This is a key workout for Champion, Cindy." Ashleigh's hazel eyes were serious. "It's his first work as a three-year-old, and we're going to see a lot about his potential today. I'm not trying to make you so tense you can't think, but some tension is good to keep you alert. As a jockey you'll be in a lot of tight situations, not only on the track but off it, too." Ashleigh smiled. "I'm assuming you're still going to apply for your apprentice jockey's license next year."

"You bet." Cindy grinned. Now she knew where Ashleigh was coming from. But Cindy was sure Champion was ready to give his best effort today. She could hardly wait to get out on the track and see how fast he was as a three-year-old. "Which horses do you think I'll be riding when I get my jockey's license?"

"We'll see," Ashleigh said, as Cindy had known she would. "It's too soon to tell."

I want to ride Champion in races, Cindy said to herself. *He'll be only four next year. I hope he's still racing and not injured.*

Ian walked over to Cindy, frowning. "Cindy, I

42

have to confess I was relieved when Sammy grew too big to be a jockey. A race is a different proposition from exercise riding—it's much more dangerous. You always have to be careful on the track, but especially in a race."

"I will be," Cindy assured him. She knew there were always risks riding in a pack of thundering Thoroughbreds, where a fall could mean serious injury or even death. *But there's no thrill like it!* she thought. Cindy just prayed she didn't grow taller than five foot three, the height she was now.

"We don't have to decide anything this minute." Ashleigh smiled at Cindy. "Why don't you warm Champion up, then breeze him a quarter."

Cindy nodded and gathered her reins. Champion was chomping at the bit and didn't need to be asked twice to move out at a walk.

Cindy saw that Saturday Special, a tall gray filly, was still out on the track, ridden by Mark. Cindy guessed that Ashleigh had asked Mark to exercise the filly late in the morning, after the other horses had gone in, to keep Champion company.

Champion's been good about working with other horses—except when Freedom and Vic go by, Cindy thought, feeling uneasy. She still wasn't sure how serious Champion's problem was. *Maybe he just has strong likes and dislikes and that's the end of it,* she hoped.

Champion pulled hard on the reins. "Yes, we've

got work to do." Cindy erased all thoughts of what could go wrong from her mind and concentrated on her riding.

She warmed the colt up at a walk and trot, then put him into a slow gallop. Mark rode up beside them on Saturday Special. Champion eyed the filly, but his ears stayed up.

"Good, Champion," Cindy praised. "Just pretend Saturday is a tree—a moving tree—and leave her alone."

"Some tree." Mark laughed.

"Whatever works!" Cindy called.

As they approached the quarter pole she gradually asked Champion to go faster. The colt responded instantly, drawing off from Saturday Special.

Cindy shook back her hair and breathed deeply. The air was icy, and she could feel her cheeks begin to burn. But the morning was beautiful. The gray clouds that hovered earlier were breaking up, and a bright band of blue showed on the horizon.

She gathered her reins, ready to ask Champion for all the speed he had. "Let's do it, boy," she whispered. "Run faster than you ever did!"

Champion's gallop quickened and his hooves plunged deeper into the harrowed dirt of the track. The quarter pole flashed by. "Now!" Cindy cried. "Go, Champion!"

The big colt roared into higher gear, like a jet screaming into the blue sky. Cindy buried her face and hands in Champion's neck, moving in time to the quick staccato of his strides. Tears from the cold filled her eyes, and the ground was a blur.

Champion was fast as a two-year-old, but he's way beyond fast now! Cindy thought blissfully. *He's an absolute powerhouse!*

Within seconds they roared past the gap. "You did it, boy!" Cindy gasped, rising in the stirrups. "I don't know what the time was, but it was plenty fast!"

The dark colt arched his neck, fighting against her restraint. "That's enough, Champion." But Cindy let him gallop out a little farther than she had intended. She didn't want to frustrate him after he had just put in a run like that.

After a few more big strides Champion decided to listen. Huffing out a sharp snort, as if he didn't care for her words, he dropped back into a trot. Cindy circled him and rode over to the gap.

Ashleigh was grinning. She held up the stopwatch. "Twenty-one and change for the quarter."

"Incredible, boy!" Cindy was beaming. "You're going to make us all so proud in the Fountain of Youth."

Champion eyed her backward and lightly pawed the ground. He seemed to be saying, *I'm ready right now.*

"I sure think his performance will be one to watch," Ashleigh agreed. "It will be like seeing Pride run again. Champion's following right in his footsteps, running in the Fountain of Youth and Florida Derby."

45

"I don't see what can go wrong." Cindy was silent for a moment. She didn't want to be overconfident, because a lot could go wrong in a horserace. Horses got jammed up in traffic on the track, or they couldn't handle the track surface, or they were injured. But she still thought Champion's chances were great in the Fountain of Youth.

"He didn't bother Saturday Special, either," Ashleigh said. "I was glad to see that."

He never bothers her because he kind of likes her. Cindy frowned slightly. *He doesn't hate her the way he does Freedom.*

She shrugged. Champion's dislike for Freedom was probably no big deal. Ashleigh, Ian, and Mike were all aware of it. At Gulfstream, Freedom would be stabled a safe distance from Champion. They would be in the same barn, but they wouldn't be neighbors.

"Good job, Cindy," Mike said.

"Thanks. Come on, Champion," Cindy said happily. "Let's cool you out. Maybe we can go for a nice walk this afternoon." After Champion's strenuous exercise that morning Cindy wouldn't ride him again that day, but Champion always enjoyed an outing on a lead line.

She took the colt up to the barn and covered him with a deep maroon blanket that she had picked out for him at the tack store. The color went well with his mahogany coat, she thought. Cindy carefully cooled Champion out, walking him around and around the stable yard. Then she put the colt in his stall.

Champion whinnied indignantly as she shut the door behind him.

"I'll take you out to the paddock in a little while," Cindy said. "But I want you to wear the blanket until then so you don't get chilled. Champion, it's your own fault you can't go out in the paddock with a blanket on. Remember what you did to the last two blankets?"

Champion pushed against the stall door, but Cindy ignored him. The last two times she had put the colt out when he was blanketed, he had somehow managed to get the blankets off. That wasn't supposed to be possible—the blankets were designed to stay on—but Champion had done it handily, ripping the straps as cleanly as if he'd cut them with scissors.

Cindy had no idea if Champion had decided to take off the blankets because he had gotten hot or he'd just decided to have some fun. One blanket had been tossed on top of a fencepost with a huge rip in the side. The other blanket ended up in the mud, trampled and ruined.

The big, well-made horse blankets were expensive, and Ian and Mike hadn't been happy about the colt's latest habit. So these days Cindy took off the blanket before she put Champion out in the paddock. He had grown a thick winter coat, and he seemed warm and perfectly happy outside without a blanket.

Ashleigh walked over to Champion's stall. "How did he come out of the workout?" she asked.

Cindy smiled, flattered that Ashleigh trusted her judgment. "Just fine. He's ready for more."

Ashleigh rubbed Champion's neck while she looked him over. Champion nodded gently, as if he were trying to persuade her to let him out since Cindy refused to. "I didn't expect anything else," Ashleigh admitted. "It's wonderful that Champion is so sound. I've started to take it for granted, but I really shouldn't. I never did with Mr. Wonderful. But of course he was already injured before the Triple Crown races."

Cindy nodded. She still felt bad that Mr. Wonderful wouldn't be racing that year. "Is there a chance you'll put him back in training?" she asked.

Champion pushed Ashleigh, as if he couldn't stand for the conversation to be about any horse but himself. Cindy quickly rubbed his muzzle to distract him.

Ashleigh sighed. "I don't think so, Cindy. Mr. Wonderful is a great competitor, and I hate to retire him from the sport. But his leg trouble could flare up again, and he might be seriously injured. And the virus may have weakened him, too. I think it's time to keep him home."

Cindy couldn't argue with that. "Whitebrook has a lot of stallions," she said, listing them on her fingers. "Wonder's Pride, Jazzman, Maxwell, Blues King, Sadler's Station, Glory, and now Mr. Wonderful."

"Well, we'll sell Sadler's Station to make room for Mr. Wonderful." Ashleigh frowned. "Sadler's offspring never did much at the track. I'm very sorry to see him go, but it's possible he'll have a future in eventing or as a pleasure horse."

Maybe Mandy would like to buy him! Cindy thought. She pictured her friend careening around a jump course on the enormous, high-powered racehorse. *I'd be afraid to suggest it—what if Mandy took me up on it?* Cindy sighed. She knew she would miss Sadler.

"I'd better get back to work," Ashleigh said. "Thanks for that great ride on Champion this morning, Cindy."

"Thanks for letting me ride," Cindy said shyly. She hoped she did good work with the horses, but she never took her opportunities for granted. She knew that not many fourteen-year-old girls got the chance to ride a stableful of gorgeous Thoroughbreds every day.

Cindy followed Ashleigh out of the barn, intending to visit Glory for a few minutes before she headed up to the cottage to clean her room. Cindy had seen earlier that Glory and Wonder's Pride were each out in side paddocks, not far from the training track.

"Hey, you guys!" she called.

The stallions' lovely heads jerked up, and both horses stared at her. Pride, with his copper-colored coat and wide-set, beautiful eyes, bore the stamp of his dam, Ashleigh's Wonder. Glory's gray head was classically sculpted, like a Roman chariot horse's.

Glory whinnied softly. "Okay, I'll come see you first," Cindy said. She walked over to Glory's paddock, trying to ignore the look of reproach in Pride's dark eyes. Glory eagerly hopped up and down on his front hooves as she approached. Cindy climbed up on the bottom board of the fence, and Glory pushed his head happily under her arm.

"So what do you think of your newest baby?" Cindy asked. Zero's Flight, Glory's second foal, had been born two days earlier. The foal, a chestnut colt, had come right on time. He was already almost as big as Glory's Joy, who was over three weeks old.

Glory rubbed his ears on her shoulder. He seemed to be saying that he didn't need any new reason to feel important.

Cindy leaned over the fence to touch her cheek to Glory's gray neck. She loved the tickle of his fur and his healthy, clean horse smell. She would have known which horse he was in the complete dark.

Glory sighed contentedly, but Pride blew out a sharp snort of exasperation. "Oh, all right, Pride." Cindy gave Glory a final pat and hurried over to the other stallion.

Pride bobbed his head repeatedly, as if to say, *About time.*

"Oh, don't pretend you don't get any attention," Cindy scolded as she rubbed the big horse's ears. "I know Ashleigh and Samantha come out here and spoil you all the time."

Cindy looked thoughtfully at Pride. It was hard to

50

imagine a prettier horse, but Pride's first crop of foals hadn't done that well at the track so far. *Of course, they're only two-year-olds,* she thought. *Pride's foals may just be slow to mature. They might do great this year as three-year-olds. After all, Pride won the Kentucky Derby. I bet his foals will be fast.*

Cindy knew that her dad, Ashleigh, and Mike weren't sure whether Pride had been bred to the right mares the previous year. Even with high-class mares, sometimes the breeding lines just didn't mesh. Whitebrook didn't own any of Pride's offspring yet. Of the two Whitebrook mares he had been bred to last year, one hadn't conceived and the other had lost her foal.

"I'm going to see the foals now," Cindy told Pride. "You'll just have to rough it for half an hour or so, until Sammy or somebody shows up to give you an apple."

As Cindy walked over to the foals' paddock both stallions whinnied loudly. Cindy grinned.

In the large front paddock the twelve mothers were searching out the first bits of green grass in the brown field. Five foals had been born so far, and the three older ones, including Glory's Joy, were frisking around the paddock.

Cindy laughed aloud as Glory's Joy zoomed across the paddock, her short tail high over her back. The filly suddenly stopped short at the rumble of a tractor starting up near the barns. The small foal fled to her mother and hid behind her, trembling.

The two newest foals, including Zero's Flight, stood quietly by their mothers. They still seemed bewildered by the bright sights and noises of the world.

Cindy opened the paddock gate and slowly walked over to Heavenly Choir and Glory's Joy. The gray mare watched her calmly. Cindy helped bring in the mares almost every night for their dinner, and she visited them often. The mares all knew her and associated her with caresses and feeding.

Cindy dropped to her knees next to Glory's Joy. The almost black foal had recovered from her fright and was nudging her mother's flank. "You are just the prettiest baby," Cindy said softly.

The foal nuzzled her trustingly, her tiny, whiskery muzzle tickling Cindy's hands. She seemed to like people already. That was a good sign. Cindy knew her dad and Mike thought Joy was completely normal, even though she had been born early, and well conformed. They were more worried about Zero's Flight, whose front legs seemed to knee in a little.

Cindy sat back on her heels and frowned. *I hope Glory's babies are winners on the track,* she thought. *If they aren't, will we have to sell him, like Sadler's Station?*

Glory's Joy looked at Cindy affectionately and stepped closer, pushing Cindy's leg with her tiny muzzle. Cindy lovingly tickled the baby's nose. "No, I don't think you'll fit in my lap, even though you're small," she said with a laugh. *Joy's small now, but she probably won't stay that way,* Cindy thought. *And size isn't everything in a racehorse. The will to win is what counts.*

"It'll be two years before you and Glory's other sons and daughters even race, so I'm not going to worry," Cindy said, gently hugging the little foal. "Right now you look perfect to me."

5

"ARE YOU READY?" HEATHER ASKED CINDY ON A SATURDAY night two weeks later. The girls were at Cindy's house, getting ready for the school dance. Heather stepped outside the upstairs bathroom and tapped her foot impatiently.

"I don't know." Cindy stared in the mirror, trying to calm the butterflies in her stomach. *I wish I wasn't always nervous before dances*, she thought. *I mean, this isn't the first one I ever went to.*

Beth had pulled back Cindy's hair in a sleek French braid. Cindy wore a black velvet dress that swept almost to her ankles, and the deep color made her brown eyes look darker. Beth had told her that she looked very pretty.

I think I look weird. Do I have on too much makeup? Cindy frowned and leaned closer to the mirror again.

"Come on, Cindy; you're taking all night," Heather insisted. "Max and Doug are downstairs waiting for us."

Cindy felt even more nervous. She glanced at Heather in the mirror. Heather's pale, blond looks were set off by a dark green crepe dress and just a touch of makeup on her eyes and lips. "Well, you look great, anyhow," Cindy said.

"Oh, so do you, but you're never happy with how you look." Heather giggled. "Maybe we should have cut up one of Champion's old blankets and made you a dress out of it. You might like that."

"Maybe." Cindy had to smile. She stood up, pushing back a tendril of her blond hair. Beth had arranged small curls around her face. *Ready or not, here I go*, she thought.

"I wonder if we'll win anything in the raffle tonight," Heather said as they walked down the stairs.

"Probably not—I bet a lot of people will be at the dance." Cindy concentrated on picking up her skirt so that she didn't trip on it. "I don't even know all the prizes that are being raffled off," she added. "I guess the committee decided on the prizes when I was so busy with Champion right before he left."

"You must miss him," Heather said sympathetically.

"Yeah, I really do." Cindy stopped on the staircase and sighed. "He's been gone two weeks, and he won't be home until after the Florida Derby in the middle of March. That's more than a month."

"Is he doing okay?" Heather asked.

"Yeah, Ashleigh says he's fine." Cindy knew that Champion wasn't nearly as sensitive as Storm or Glory had been. Ashleigh understood that Champion liked a lot of attention, and she would be sure to give him what he needed to run his best.

"Are you guys coming down?" Max called.

Cindy started. Max and Doug Mellinger stood at the bottom of the stairs, smiling up at them. Doug and Heather had a comfortable relationship similar to Cindy and Max's.

Max looks so cute all dressed up, Cindy thought. "We were talking about horses!" She hurried down the stairs, almost catching her foot on her skirt.

"You look great," Max said. He seemed a little embarrassed.

"Thanks, so do you." Cindy smoothed her dress, trying not to sound as flustered as she felt.

Beth popped her head in from the kitchen. Ian and Samantha were behind her.

"You look beautiful, sweetheart," Ian said.

"You really do." Samantha smiled encouragingly.

"I want to take a picture before you go," Beth said.

"Mom!" Cindy rolled her eyes. She hated to have her picture taken.

"Just one." Beth lifted her camera. "Stand over by the fireplace, all of you."

All four friends walked to the fireplace and put their arms around each other. Cindy tried to smile naturally, but she doubted if she was successful. *I'm not very photogenic*, she thought.

Beth snapped the picture and lowered the camera. "Why don't you all sit on the couch now?"

"You said just one picture!" Cindy protested.

"Come on, Cindy," Beth said firmly. "You'll thank me someday."

"Maybe in twenty years," Cindy mumbled, carefully tucking her dress under her on the couch.

"Smile, Cindy," Ian called.

"Think about Glory's Joy," Samantha said encouragingly.

Cindy smiled, remembering the small, beautiful foal. She jumped when the camera flash went off. *I bet Beth got a decent picture of me for once,* she thought.

As Beth drove the foursome to the gym Cindy talked with her friends about Champion, forgetting her worries about the way she looked. Beth dropped them off in front of the school.

"I'll pick you up at eleven," she said. "Have a great time."

"We will!" Cindy could feel her excitement mounting as she looked around at the brightly lit school. Small groups of kids and couples, laughing and talking, were approaching the gym.

Just inside the gym Cindy filled out a raffle ticket. "Number eighty-nine," she said. "Wow, a lot of people bought tickets."

"There's four of us, so somebody might win a prize," Doug said.

"Cindy! Why don't you guys come sit with us?" Laura Billings called from one of the tables set up in the gym.

Cindy and her friends joined Laura, Sharon, and their dates, Joe Exton and Kyle Payton. The tables were set with small baskets of chips, bowls of dip, and pitchers of punch. On the walls were painted winter scenes of ice skaters sailing across the ice, and the floor glittered with a dusting of artificial snow. "Hey, this dance is really fancy—who thought up all this?" Cindy teased.

"A bunch of geniuses." Max grinned. "Do you want to dance?"

"Sure." Cindy had never thought she would be a good dancer, but to her surprise, that year she had discovered that she wasn't bad. The different rhythms of the music seemed similar to the different gaits of a horse. It wasn't much harder for her to stay in time to the music than to ride.

As she and Max whirled around the floor with the other dancers, Cindy felt like she was at an ice-skating rink. *Heather really is a genius*, she thought looking over at her friend. Heather was out on the dance floor, too, chatting with Doug.

"It's time for the raffle," Max said after he and Cindy had danced several dances. "I have to go." He pointed at a podium that several ninth graders were dragging onto the dance floor. "I was elected master of ceremonies at our last committee meeting."

"I'll go back to our table," Cindy said, smiling. She took a seat with Heather, Doug, and Laura and looked expectantly up at Max. A hush fell over the room.

"This is going to be good," Heather whispered to Cindy. "Wait till you see what the prizes are."

Max fished in a big glass jar. "We have ten prizes to give away," he announced. "The first prize is a ride on a Whitebrook Thoroughbred, donated by Cindy McLean. It goes to—" Max pulled out a slip of paper—"Chelsea Billings!"

"That's my little sister," Laura exclaimed. "She's going to scream with joy when she hears about this—talk about a horse nut!" Laura got up. "I'll get the prize for her."

Cindy watched Laura claim her prize, then relaxed in her seat again. She and Heather smiled at each other. *This is fun!* Cindy thought to herself.

Max reached into the jar again. "And the next prize goes to . . . Cindy McLean!"

Cindy sat up straight, startled. *I wonder what I won!* she thought excitedly.

"Cindy's prize is an all-expenses paid cat from the animal shelter," Max called as Cindy made her way to the podium.

Cool! Cindy smiled broadly as she took her certificate from Max. Whitebrook had a lot of cats, but Cindy had never gotten to pick out a special cat of her own. She couldn't wait to go to the animal shelter.

The rest of the dance passed in a happy blur for Cindy. Max asked her to dance almost every dance, but several other boys from her class asked her, too. Before that night, Cindy had always been too shy to dance with boys she didn't know well.

Max is definitely the cutest guy here, she thought as she danced with Gary Caldwell, a tenth grader. Max was drinking punch near the refreshment table, but Cindy saw that he was looking back at her. *I hope he thinks my dancing is okay*, Cindy worried.

Max walked over to Cindy and Gary. "Can I cut in?" he asked over the music. "This is one of my favorite songs."

"Sure," Gary said. "If Cindy doesn't mind."

"I don't." Cindy smiled into Max's green eyes as they began to dance to the slow old sixties song. "I like alternative music, but this is nice, too," she said. *Kind of romantic!* she added to herself.

Max nodded, and Cindy rested her head lightly on his shoulder. Colored spotlights whirled before her eyes, turning the glitter on the floor brilliant green, red, and gold. Cindy could hardly believe how wonderful this evening was.

All too soon it was eleven o'clock and time to go home. A light dusting of snow had begun to sift out of the black sky as Cindy walked with Max and her other friends to Beth's car. Cindy held Max's arm so she wouldn't slip.

"That was our best dance yet," Heather said after they were all settled in the car.

"The very best," Cindy agreed, tilting her head back to watch the snow come down through the rear window. She could still hear in her mind the sixties song she and Max had slow danced to. Max was quiet, too, as if he had a lot to think about.

Cindy was dropped off first at Whitebrook. Max walked her to the door, then hesitated. *Why isn't he looking at me?* Cindy wondered.

"Thanks for coming to the dance with me," Max said, finally glancing in her direction.

Cindy smiled. "I loved it."

The snow had begun to come down heavily, and Cindy could feel the cold flakes sticking to her eyelashes. She blinked them off, enjoying the wet cool on her face.

Max looked back at the car, where their friends were waiting. He frowned, then cupped his hands in the soft snow to make a snowball.

"Don't throw that—" Cindy began in a teasing voice.

Max abruptly dropped the snowball. He looked straight at her, his green eyes very bright.

Cindy stopped breathing as Max leaned forward and his lips touched hers in the gentlest of kisses. "Good night," he said softly, and turned to leave.

Max kissed me! Cindy thought, her eyes wide. Her heart was hammering in her chest. "Good night," she called.

Cindy slipped into the house and leaned against the door, pressing her flushed face against its cool surface.

"Do friends kiss, or does this make us more than friends?" she murmured. "I'm not sure. But I do know that was really, really nice."

Max kissed me, Max kissed me, Max kissed me, Cindy sang blissfully to herself as she walked upstairs to bed. She doubted if she would sleep for a long time.

"There's Mandy," Samantha said the next morning. She and Cindy were just finishing brunch in the kitchen.

Cindy leaned around her sister and saw the Jarvises' car and horse trailer pulling up the drive. Cindy had invited her friend over to Whitebrook for a trail ride, and Mandy's father had agreed to trailer over Butterball for the day. "Great—now we can get started," she said.

Cindy was looking forward to riding with Mandy. Mandy liked to go for long, hard rides, like she did.

Besides, I haven't seen Mandy in a week, Cindy thought as she gulped down the rest of her grapefruit juice and hurried to the hall to grab a coat. With Mandy's schedule of jumping lessons and Cindy's chores at Whitebrook, neither girl had much time left over.

Who should I ride today? Cindy wondered. She quickly shut the cottage door and jumped over the stoop to avoid the drips of melting snow coming from the roof.

Since Champion was at the track, that morning Cindy had exercise ridden Freedom's Ring. *Freedom isn't nearly as exciting to ride as Champion*, she thought. *But riding him was good experience. For months I've hardly ridden anybody except Champion.* When Champion was at Whitebrook, the talented, headstrong colt monopolized almost all Cindy's time. But Cindy knew that as a jockey she would be expected to ride many mounts, sometimes in a single day.

"Hi, Cindy!" Mandy called, backing Butterball out of the horse trailer. Mr. Jarvis unhitched the trailer from the car.

Cindy hurried over to her friend. Mandy had already clipped the butterscotch-colored pony to a ring on the horse trailer. She was searching in the front tack compartment for her saddle and bridle.

Mr. Jarvis waved to Cindy. "I'll see you later, sweetie," he said to Mandy as he started the car. "Be careful."

"I always am," Mandy said cheerfully.

Mandy does reckless things, but she's careful while she does them, Cindy thought. *I guess that counts as being careful.*

Butterball shook his mane and peered at Cindy through his thick forelock. "He's got the right kind of coat for today," Cindy said, patting the pony's heavy coat. The morning was gray and chilly, but the weak winter sun was trying to come out. Small white

63

patches of snow sprinkled the wet brown grass in the paddocks.

"Yeah, Butter's always warm." Mandy was already saddling the pony. "I don't even have a blanket for him."

Butterball twisted his small head around and affectionately butted Mandy. "Are you really going to look for another horse?" Cindy asked.

"I guess. I asked Tor to look for one. But I don't want another horse unless my parents will let me keep Butter." For a moment Mandy's big brown eyes were stricken. "I think they will, but I'm afraid to ask."

"I don't blame you. Guess what—I'm getting another animal, too," Cindy said. "At the dance last night I won a cat from the shelter!"

"Oh, cool!" Mandy said excitedly. "Let's go get it today!"

"I want to, if I can get someone to drive me over there," Cindy responded.

"Are you going to ride double with me on Butter or are you going to saddle up somebody?" Mandy asked with a giggle.

"I have to decide who to saddle up." Cindy grinned. "I bet Butter could carry both of us, though. Ponies are strong."

From one of the front paddocks Glory whinnied to Butterball. The small pony was instantly alert. He pricked his ears, stamped impatiently, and strained against the lead rope toward Glory.

"Butter's full of himself this morning," Cindy said.

"Yeah." Mandy was gazing at the far paddocks, but she wasn't looking at Glory.

"Who are you looking for?" Cindy asked.

"Oh, nobody. I know Sierra's at Tor's for the winter, but I wish I could ride him," Mandy said, referring to Whitebrook's world-class steeplechaser. Sierra spent winters at the Nelsons' stable, where he could be exercised over jumps indoors.

Cindy stared at her friend in amazement. Sierra was a temperamental, full-size horse. "Dream on, Mandy," she said. "Sierra's a long way from Butterball. For one thing, Sierra is about five hands taller than Butter. And he may be incredibly talented, but he's also incredibly hard to ride."

"I am dreaming on," Mandy insisted. "I've decided what kind of new horse I want."

"What kind?" Cindy looked at her friend expectantly.

"A Thoroughbred, of course," Mandy answered. "They're the fastest."

"They're also the hottest blooded and hardest to control." But Cindy could see why Mandy wanted a Thoroughbred. *I can't talk her out of getting one anyway,* she thought. *Mandy never listens to anybody. It's no wonder Mandy likes Sierra—she's as headstrong as he is. Come to think of it, they both have the same aggressive style of jumping.*

"I know Thoroughbreds are hard to ride," Mandy

admitted. She ruffled Butterball's thick mane. "But if I could control a Thoroughbred, that would be the best kind of horse for me to have. So I'll try."

Mandy always tries her hardest, Cindy thought. She had to admire Mandy's decision. After all, Cindy rode Thoroughbreds herself, despite the risks. She wouldn't trade a ride on a Thoroughbred for anything.

"Why don't you ride Wonder?" Mandy asked.

"I've never ridden her. Only Ashleigh does." Cindy thought a moment. The paddocks were full of lively Thoroughbreds, all eager for an outing. "I'll take Glory," she said. Cindy felt a little guilty about giving Glory another ride. Most of the other horses got out a lot less than he did. But she couldn't resist the idea of a wonderful ride on her beloved big gray stallion.

Mandy looked at Cindy and hesitated. "Can I ride one of the Whitebrook horses, too? Just for the first part of the ride," she said quickly. "Then I'll ride Butter."

"Who do you want to ride?" Cindy looked at Mandy in surprise.

"Well, out in the paddock I just saw that jumper Tor is keeping here," Mandy said.

"Yeah . . ." Cindy hesitated. Tor had brought the horse, Far Sailor, over to Whitebrook the previous week. The weather had been good, and he had wanted to work Far Sailor over the jumps set up on the Whitebrook turf course.

"I'd like to ride Far Sailor—since Sierra's not around," Mandy said.

Cindy couldn't tell if Mandy was joking or not. "We'll have to ask somebody if you can ride Sailor."

"Okay," Mandy said eagerly.

Samantha was working on a computer in the stable office. "I don't know about this," she said when she heard Mandy's plan. "I know you've been riding full size horses at Tor's, but Sailor's so big and strong. That's what makes him a good jumper, but—"

"We're just going for a trail ride." Cindy didn't want Mandy to be disappointed.

Samantha frowned in thought. "All right," she said. "But stay on the trails."

"Great!" Mandy cheered.

Cindy helped her friend tack up Far Sailor. He wasn't much over fifteen hands, and the chestnut had a gentle, intelligent expression. He was big, but only for someone as small as Mandy. *She should be able to handle him*, Cindy thought. *After all, we're only going for a trail ride.*

She got Glory out of one of the paddocks and led him to the barn. Glory was overjoyed at the prospect of a ride, and Cindy could hardly get him to hold still so that she could put on the saddle. She met Mandy in the stable yard.

"Can we go on the training track for a few minutes?" Mandy asked. "I don't think I've ever been on it."

"Sure." Cindy looked at Mandy curiously. She couldn't imagine why Mandy would want to ride there. "You're not thinking about being a jockey, are you?"

Mandy shook her head. "I did tell my parents that I planned to event, though," she said.

"I bet they weren't happy."

Mandy shook her head. "Nope. They hope I'll drop the idea."

Cindy doubted if that would happen. She had known Mandy for several years, and Mandy had never once dropped an idea.

On the training track Mandy began to circle Far Sailor at a walk, then a trot. The dirt track was wet from the melting snow, and occasionally Sailor splashed in a puddle. But Mandy seemed to have him well in hand.

Cindy stopped Glory to watch. She leaned back in the saddle and rested her hand on his rump. Glory stood comfortably on three legs. *He was a spirited, high-energy racehorse, but he's a dynamite trail horse, too,* Cindy thought fondly.

After several minutes Mandy moved Sailor to the inside turf course and stopped him. A course of jumps was still set up from Tor's work with Sailor last week.

Why did Mandy go there? Cindy wondered. *Is the dirt track too muddy?*

Mandy seemed to be talking to Sailor. Then she headed the gelding at the jumps!

"Stop," Cindy cried, sitting bolt upright. Mandy

had to be out of her mind! She was riding a strange horse at three-foot jumps on a slippery course!

Mandy cantered Sailor at the first jump, made of thick, tied-together logs. Cindy gasped as Mandy's takeoff seemed a little short. The heavy logs on the course wouldn't give if Sailor didn't take them right.

But the well-trained horse compensated with an extra effort, and he and Mandy easily made the jump. Mandy turned Sailor toward a chicken coop and blew over it.

Cindy sank back in the saddle. *If I yell at Mandy, I'll just break her concentration,* she thought. *And she's making all the jumps—at least so far.*

After four more difficult jumps Mandy pulled up Far Sailor and posted over to Cindy. She was laughing. "That was great!" she called.

Cindy felt a flash of anger. Mandy could have gotten hurt, jumping a horse as big as Sailor without supervision. Cindy would have been in major trouble. She might be anyway, if anyone had seen Mandy's performance. "Mandy, you weren't allowed to jump," Cindy said sharply.

"No one said I couldn't." Mandy grinned.

"That's only because nobody thought you would." Cindy stared accusingly at her friend. "We were supposed to go on the *trails.*"

"The track is kind of a trail," Mandy said, still grinning. "Wow! That was fun!"

"Jeez, I'm so glad." Cindy sighed and gripped

Glory's reins. Her hands were still shaking a little from stress. *I guess I should have known Mandy would do something like that,* she thought. *Nothing Mandy does on horseback should surprise me.*

After a quick lunch Samantha agreed to drive Cindy and Mandy to the animal shelter. "I've got a lot to do here, but I know you don't want to wait another second to get your new cat," she said, smiling. "I haven't completely forgotten what it's like to be a kid."

"Thanks, Sammy!" Cindy jumped up and hurried to the car, with Mandy right behind her.

The animal shelter was just outside Lexington. Cindy waited tensely while Samantha parked. Cindy could see outside runs full of dogs of different shapes and sizes, barking loudly.

"The cats are inside," Samantha said.

"How do you know?" Cindy had to shout over the noise of the dogs.

"I used to volunteer here." Samantha pointed at a low concrete building. "That's the office."

Cindy presented her gift certificate to an animal control officer, who took her back to the cat cages. Cindy walked slowly past row after row of colorful cats, each in a separate small cage. There were black cats, tiger cats, and even an elegant, blue-eyed Siamese.

"Ooh, look at this one." Mandy pointed to a lively white kitten, jumping at the wire of its cage.

"What a cutie," Cindy said. Most of the cats had come over to the front of their cages and were pawing at the wire or climbing on it. They all seemed to be begging Cindy to take them home.

Cindy's heart ached. *I can't believe no one wants these beautiful animals*, she thought. *If only I could take them all.*

Finally she had narrowed her choice to three: a friendly coal black male cat, the playful white kitten, and a small, sleek young tortoiseshell. The tortoiseshell was the only cat quietly sitting at the back of her cage. But her unblinking gray eyes followed Cindy's every move. "I can't decide," Cindy said.

"Just one, Cindy," Samantha warned. "Beth told me not to bother coming home if I've got a carload of animals."

Cindy hesitated, then held out her hand to the tortoiseshell. The little cat stepped forward without hesitation, as if she accepted Cindy's decision. "The other two cats are so nice, someone will definitely adopt them," Cindy said. "But this kitty is so shy, she might get left here."

"Good choice," Mandy approved.

Cindy filled out the paperwork in the office and carried the cat to the car. The cat settled in Cindy's arms and purred.

"What are you going to call her?" Mandy asked as Samantha backed out of the drive.

"I'm not sure yet." Cindy was surprised how calm

the cat was in the car. *She seems to trust me already*, she thought.

At Whitebrook, Cindy carried the cat out to the feed room in the training barn. Beth didn't want animals in the house, and Cindy thought the cat would be more comfortable in the barn anyway. The other cats would keep her company.

"Let's give her some milk and food," Cindy said to Mandy, cradling the kitten in her arms. "I want her to know this is home."

Mandy reached for a can of cat food on the feed room shelf and spooned the contents into a bowl. Cindy set the cat on the floor, and she eagerly but delicately began to eat.

Mandy looked out the door. "Uh-oh, here comes company," she said.

Most of the Whitebrook cats were trotting quickly down the barn aisle. Sidney, Pride's cat, was there, and so was Flurry, Shining's special friend. Imp, Glory's companion, brought up the rear.

"Do you think they'll pick on the new cat?" Mandy asked nervously.

"I don't think so," Cindy said. The tortoiseshell hiked her tail high over her back and walked back and forth, as if she were modeling for the other cats.

Sidney hissed, his black-and-white face crinkling. The two gray cats sat down and stared coldly at the newcomer.

"I don't think they like her," Mandy said.

"They just don't know her yet. Poor girl," Cindy said sympathetically, stroking her kitten's back. "I think the other cats will warm up after a while. Don't worry—I bet you'll find a special horse friend, too, just like they did."

6

JUST TWO DAYS BEFORE THE FOUNTAIN OF YOUTH STAKES Cindy stepped out of the airport into the brilliant Miami sunshine. She breathed in the sweet, warm tropical air. "The weather is wonderful!" she exclaimed.

"Hey, you don't need to convince me that Florida's great," Samantha said, propping Kevin against her hip. "I was born here, remember?" The red-haired baby twisted in her arms, as if he wanted to see the sights, too.

"You lived here for a long time, didn't you, Sammy?" Cindy asked.

Samantha looked sad. "I guess I lived here longer than anywhere else."

Cindy nodded sympathetically. *Maybe I shouldn't have brought that up*, she thought. Ian and Samantha's mother had planned to settle in Florida many years earlier, but Samantha's mother had been killed in a riding accident when Samantha was twelve. Ian and Samantha had then drifted from track to track for a long time before he finally took a job as assistant trainer at Townsend Acres.

Beth walked through the airport doors, carrying Christina. "Why are you two just standing around?" she teased. "Don't you want to get to the track?"

Samantha smiled. "You bet!" She signaled a taxi.

"I hope Champion is okay." Cindy squinted into the sunlight as they piled into the taxi. She removed a pair of sunglasses from her backpack. "I wish I didn't have school," she added. "Then I could stay with him whenever he was away from home."

"Well, you're going to have a lot more of it," Beth said firmly. "School is very important in the horse business."

"I guess." Cindy sighed. She knew that Ashleigh spent a lot of time with the horses, but she also put in many hours in the stable office, working with numbers, pedigrees, and people.

"I'll meet you at the track in a while," Beth said. "I'm going to take Kevin and Christina to the motel for a nap."

"We'll tell Dad," Samantha replied.

Cindy waved good-bye to Beth and Kevin at the motel, then looked eagerly out the taxi window, waiting for her first glimpse of the modern, elegant Gulfstream track. Florida always seemed so exotic to her with its tall palm trees and pastel colors.

"Here we are," Samantha cried as the taxi stopped at Gulfstream. She slammed the taxi door. "What are we waiting for?" she said with a grin. "Let's go see our horses!"

"Race you!" Cindy took off running for the track gate. Her heart was almost bursting with joy at the thought of seeing Champion again. She slowed to a walk as she approached the first of the neat green-and-white shed rows.

It feels good not to worry about the Whitebrook horses, she thought as she passed the first shed row. Since the horses had arrived at Gulfstream, all the reports about their workouts and general health had been positive.

A soft, scented breeze brushed back Cindy's blond hair as she reached the Whitebrook shed row. Champion, Limitless Time, and Freedom's Ring were all stabled in barn nine. "Champion!" she called. "I'm here, boy!"

A quick whinny greeted her, followed by the scrape of an impatiently pawing hoof. Cindy rushed to the colt's stall, ducking under the white sun awning that shaded the stalls.

Champion was hanging his head over the netting on his door. When he saw Cindy, he whinnied imperiously again.

"Yes, I'm back," Cindy said, laughing as she hugged his neck tight. "I missed you so much."

Cindy felt unexpected tears fill her eyes. *Champion looks so beautiful,* she thought. In the dim light Champion's coat glowed a warm chocolate, accentuating the bright blaze on his face. From the colt's feisty expression, Cindy could tell he was raring to go.

Champion stretched out his neck even farther, checking Cindy's shorts pockets for carrots.

"Oh, I'm sorry," Cindy apologized. "I was in such a hurry, I didn't have a chance to load up on carrots. I'll go get some right now." Cindy turned and bumped smack into her dad.

"Hi, Cindy," Ian said, smiling.

"Dad! You scared me," Cindy protested.

"I didn't want to interrupt your reunion." Ian laughed and hugged Cindy. "Champion looks good, doesn't he? But he did miss you. For the better part of some days he'd turn his tail toward the door and sulk. I'm glad you're here, honey."

"Me too. But Champion looks fit." Cindy's heart soared. She was sure he would win on Saturday.

Cindy fed Champion several carrots, then walked down the stable aisle to visit the rest of the Whitebrook string. Ashleigh and Samantha were in Freedom's stall, discussing his upcoming race, for nonwinners of two races, on Saturday.

"I still think he's got a lot of potential," Ashleigh said, running her hand across the colt's black back. "He's off to a slow start, but only compared to a precocious horse like Champion. Freedom's just three—we'll see how he does this year."

Cindy knew that any race at a competitive track like Gulfstream was no piece of cake. She patted the good-natured black colt's neck, silently wishing him well.

"Let's check on Limitless," Ashleigh said.

"I'm going to give Champion just one more carrot first," Cindy said. Champion was looking out of his stall, as if he hoped she would have such an idea. "Here you go," Cindy said, stretching out her hand with the carrot to him.

The big colt squealed with displeasure and bolted to the back of his stall. "Champion!" Cindy cried, startled. "What on earth is the matter?"

Champion shook his head. Then he slowly stepped to the front of the stall again and touched her hand, taking a deep sniff.

Cindy frowned. Why was Champion acting so strangely? "Oh, I bet I know," she said. "I just patted Freedom, and you can smell that on my hand. Champion, that's ridiculous. Why do you hate him so much?"

Champion rubbed his head on her hands and leaned adoringly on them. Either he agreed or he had decided to forgive her, Cindy thought. She closed her eyes and dropped her head on his neck, enjoying the clean smell of his soft fur. It felt so good to be near her horse after their long separation.

Ashleigh walked over. "Trouble?" she asked.

"Nope." Cindy opened her eyes and smiled. "Don't you think Champion is going to pound the competition on Saturday?" she asked. "He's just seems totally up for it."

"He does," Ashleigh agreed, tickling Champion's nose. "But some of horseracing is always luck and things you can't foresee. We'll just have to see how the race plays out."

On Saturday, race day, Cindy carefully watched as Champion and his competition paced by her in the walking ring. The Fountain of Youth was a prep race for the Kentucky Derby, and every year some of the country's most talented three-year-olds were entered. Cindy knew that this year the six-horse field was extremely competitive.

"Is that Duke's Devil?" Cindy asked Samantha. The powerful black colt was walking after his trainer, as calmly as an exercise pony. But with every step his muscles rippled under his shining coat. He looked highly conditioned and ready to race.

"That's him," Samantha said. "He's really grown up since he raced Champion in the Bashford and Breeders' Futurity last year."

"Champion's going in as the favorite, though," Cindy pointed out. The oddsmakers' decision to call Champion the favorite in the Fountain of Youth reflected his victories last year in the Bonus Series, Cindy was sure.

Cindy's eyes went to Champion, who was following Duke's Devil at a distance. *Champion's a perfect racehorse*, she thought, feeling a quick rush of pride as the lovely colt pranced by her. Every inch of Champion was conditioned to perfection. His deep brown coat gleamed under the bright Florida sun, and his four satiny white stockings glittered. Champion was sweating lightly in the heat, but it didn't seem to be bothering him.

Cindy saw that the colt was watching Duke's Devil, who had closed the gap between them. Champion's ears went back a fraction. "No, Champion!" Cindy muttered under her breath. "Leave him alone!" Champion definitely didn't like the black colt. Before the Bashford Stakes the previous summer Champion had actually tried to attack him.

Len quickly jiggled Champion's lead line to distract him. The colt's ears relaxed. He seemed to have thought the better of going after Duke's Devil. "Good." Cindy breathed a sigh of relief.

"Champion seems to have grown out of fighting with other horses in the walking ring," Samantha said.

"I'm still glad Secret Sign and Shawn Biermont aren't here, though," Cindy answered. Champion had beaten the other colt in the Kentucky

Cup Juvenile Stakes and the Breeders' Futurity the previous fall, but the Secret Sign's jockey, Shawn Biermont, had whipped Champion during one of the races. When Ashleigh had protested at the end of the race, Shawn had pretended he did it because Champion was threatening his colt.

"Whitebrook's on a roll!" Beth called from behind Cindy. Beth stood behind several rows of people, holding Kevin.

Cindy grinned and turned to flash Beth a *V* for victory sign. Cindy knew that her mom was referring to Limitless Time's three-length win in his allowance race earlier that day. Freedom had run well in his race the day before, too, taking second in a ten-horse field in his nonwinners-of-two race.

The call came for riders up, and Len took Champion over to Ashleigh. Cindy and Samantha hurried to join them.

Champion eyed Cindy brightly and tossed his head. He was an old hand at racing now, and he seemed to know just what was ahead of him. "Atta boy," Cindy said, patting the colt's velvet nose.

"Here we go," Ashleigh said. "Champion's first race of his three-year-old season." Cindy saw that Ashleigh was smiling, but her jaw was set. Cindy remembered what Ashleigh had told her about tense situations for jockeys. The Kentucky Derby was still more than two months away, but the eyes of the Thoroughbred world were on this race.

"Good luck." Cindy looked up at Ashleigh.

Ashleigh smiled and gathered her reins. "I think we'll have it today."

Champion stepped out quickly for the track, as if he couldn't wait to get started. Cindy felt a momentary stab of jealousy as she watched Ashleigh ride him into the tunnel. With only a little over a year to go until her sixteenth birthday, Cindy wished more than ever that she could ride Champion in a race.

Cindy dug her hands into her pockets and reminded herself to be patient. *No one could do a better job of riding Champion than Ashleigh,* she reminded herself as she walked to the stands with Beth, Kevin, Ian, and Mike.

Cindy watched tensely as the horses loaded in the gate, praying they would all go in quickly. Champion had loaded second, and she hoped he wouldn't have to stand long. The colt might get fidgety and break badly.

Today the horses were on their best behavior and went straight into the gate. They waited quietly under the hot blue sky for the bell.

At the abrupt, shrill sound the horses broke in a jumble of brown, black, and gray bodies. Cindy quickly searched for Champion in the clouds of dust, her heart thumping.

"Ashleigh's got him clear and he's on the lead!" Mike said with relief.

"Yes!" Cindy let out her breath in a whoosh. Champion was running strongly on the rail, his almost black mane and tail streaming.

"It's Wonder's Champion on the lead by half a length, back two to Cool Swing; CanIDoIt is up close third, followed by Dare to Love and Fantail, neck and neck," the announcer called. "Duke's Devil trails by seven as they pass the stands for the first time."

The horses plunged into the first turn with Champion on the lead. *Now if he can just keep it*, Cindy thought. The race was a mile and a sixteenth, around two turns. That left plenty of time for other horses in the field to challenge.

"Champion needs to open up a little distance on the field," Ian said. "Now, Ashleigh!"

As if she had heard, Ashleigh let Champion out a notch. The colt's fluid strides became longer as he reached for ground. He drew away by three lengths as he pounded across the backstretch.

"Perfect, Champion," Cindy cried. "Just keep it up!"

"I hope he can—he's setting fast fractions," Mike said anxiously.

Cindy swallowed hard, rapidly scanning the field. She could hardly bear the thought that Champion could lead almost the entire race, then be caught near the wire. But to her relief she saw that the other horses were well back. CanIDoIt was trailing by four lengths and Duke's Devil by five. None of the other horses seemed in contention.

"The field is turning for home," the announcer called. "It's still Wonder's Champion; back five to CanIDoIt. CanIDoIt is fading. But here comes Duke's Devil on the outside, making a late run! He's narrowed the gap to Wonder's Champion to two lengths—a length. They're coming down to the final furlong!"

"No!" Cindy whispered, jumping to her feet. Duke's Devil was still cutting into Champion's lead, until the colts were almost neck and neck. The wire was just ahead!

Champion bore out slightly. He seemed to be watching the other colt.

"Leave him alone, Champion," Cindy gasped. "You've got to run for your life!"

In a heartstopping moment she saw that she would get her wish. Champion abruptly changed gears again. He was going faster—so fast, no horse in the world could catch him! "That's it, boy!" she screamed. "Do it—you're wonderful!"

Champion lunged ahead of the other colt, his strides huge as he pounded for the wire.

"And it's Wonder's Champion by one and driving," the announcer called. "A colt to watch for in the Derby, everyone."

Cindy let out a whoop, and she hugged Samantha. "Let's go congratulate Ashleigh!" Cindy said.

Ashleigh swung out of the saddle just as Cindy walked up to the gap. She gave Cindy a high five and winked. "Nothing to it today," she said.

"Good job, Champion," Cindy praised. The colt's dark neck glistened with sweat, but she was glad to see he was breathing easily. He seemed to have come out of the race fine.

Champion lowered his head to Cindy's hands and whuffed. He permitted her to rub his blaze but then jumped sideways with a loud snort.

"No, Champion—you're not going out on the track again!" Cindy said happily. "I think you've done enough for today."

"That was a textbook race," Ian said, smiling broadly.

"Champion ran a great one today," Ashleigh agreed. "I really didn't have any problems out there with traffic, either."

"And the weather was perfect," Mike said. "Champion likes a dry, fast track."

"Thank goodness there weren't any accidents," Beth added.

Cindy barely heard them. Her mind was still filled with the beauty of Champion's charge for the wire. Champion was jerking repeatedly at the reins, as if to say, *Aren't I a fine fellow?*

"You're wonderful, boy," Cindy assured him. "Absolutely the best!" All her Kentucky Derby dreams were alive again, burning in her brain. Cindy remembered Wonder's gallant drive in the stretch of the Kentucky Derby years earlier as she overpowered a field of colts. Pride had blazed across the finish in his Derby win, taking two-fifths of a second off the track record.

I wonder what Champion's Derby will be like? Cindy thought, grinning happily. *If he runs the way he just did, we're going to see a fantastic show.*

7

CINDY RETURNED TO WHITEBROOK LATE SUNDAY NIGHT, leaving Champion at Gulfstream. She hated to be separated from the colt again, but she knew it wasn't fair to leave Len short-handed at the farm for so long.

Cindy had stayed late at Champion's stall on Sunday, petting and praising him so that he would know just how well he had done. The colt had definitely gotten the message. Cindy had spoiled him so much, he wouldn't let her leave the stall for a minute without whinnying sharply in protest.

The next morning at school Cindy was still tired from the Florida trip and the excitement. Yawning, she pulled her books out of her locker. *Maybe I can just have a quiet day, then go home and take a nap,* she thought.

Then she remembered that she couldn't. Today Laura's little sister, Chelsea, was coming over to Whitebrook for the Thoroughbred ride she had won in the raffle.

"Cindy!" Looking down the hall, Cindy saw Heather, Laura, Melissa, and Sharon walking toward her. "Tell us all about the race!"

"Champion won," Cindy said with a big smile, forgetting how tired she was.

"We know that—I thought you were going to call me last night," Heather complained.

"I was, but I didn't get home until midnight," Cindy said. She quickly sketched out the details of Champion's win as she and her friends walked to their first-period classes.

"When do you go back to Gulfstream?" Laura asked.

"Not for almost three weeks—I'll fly down just before the Florida Derby, on March 16. My parents say I can catch up with my homework in the meantime." Cindy shrugged. "I'd like to go down earlier, but I'm glad I'll be back with him right before the next race."

"You said he was doing fine, though, right?" Heather said.

"He is. But I miss him." Cindy also missed being at the track. She loved the excitement there, from the preparations to make the horses look their finest to the thrilling moments of the races.

"Chelsea will be over at four, okay?" Laura asked. "She hasn't talked about anything else for days."

"I'll be ready," Cindy promised.

"Social committee meeting after school," Melissa said. "We're going to start planning the end-of-school dance."

"I'd better not come to that today since Chelsea's coming over." Cindy wanted to get home a little early and pick just the right horse for her guest to ride. *After all, your first ride on a Thoroughbred is a really big deal,* she thought. *I want to make it something Chelsea will remember the rest of her life.*

Chelsea showed up at Whitebrook that afternoon at ten minutes till four. She ran over to the paddock, where Cindy was petting Shining. "Wow, who's that?" she asked eagerly.

"Shining," Cindy said with a smile. "And I'm Cindy."

Chelsea blushed. "Sorry," she said. "I'm Chelsea."

Cindy laughed. "I figured that out."

Chelsea climbed up on the fence. Her eyes roamed over the paddocks, taking in the dozens of sleek Thoroughbreds grazing the first shoots of spring grass. "I can't believe you live here with all these horses," she said, sounding awed.

"Sometimes I can't believe it, either." Cindy leaned over the fence next to Chelsea. "So which horse do you like?"

"Can I ride any one I want?" Chelsea asked eagerly.

"No, we have to pick a horse that's exactly right

for you." Cindy studied her small visitor, who was gently patting Shining's black nose. Chelsea was small and slender. She had a mop of curly dark hair and gray-blue eyes and looked about ten years old. "How much riding experience have you had?" Cindy asked.

"Not much." Chelsea looked downcast. "My father trains at the Souters', but my parents say I'm too young to exercise ride over there. We don't have any horses at our place. He says we can't afford one."

"That's too bad. But I didn't have a horse either when I was your age, so don't give up hope," Cindy said.

Glory snorted loudly from his paddock. The gray stallion was watching the action from his paddock. He looked indignant that he wasn't the focus of attention.

"I'll ride that one," Chelsea said quickly.

Cindy tried not to laugh. Even though Chelsea didn't know Glory, he hardly looked like a tame pleasure horse. *But he is beautiful*, she reminded herself. *That's probably why Chelsea picked him.* "Glory's a stallion," she said. "He's a really nice one—he's my special horse, and I helped train him. But he's kind of a one-person horse. I wouldn't recommend that you take him on one of your very first rides."

"Are all the horses really sensitive?" Chelsea asked.

"That's almost a rule with racehorses." Cindy thought a moment.

"How about Ruling Spirit?" she suggested. "He's the almost black horse over there with the other geldings." Cindy pointed to one of the back paddocks. "My friend Max rides him a lot when he comes over. Spirit's gentle, but he's got some get up and go."

"He's gorgeous," Chelsea said. "I'd love to ride him."

She's not hard to please! Cindy thought. She already liked the younger girl. "We use Spirit to help exercise the horses in training," Cindy said as she led the way to the paddock.

"I want to be an exercise rider," Chelsea said firmly.

"Well, Spirit might be a good horse for you to start on. He can teach you things." Cindy walked over to the gelding and slipped on a halter. "Do you want to lead him up to the barn?"

"Sure." Chelsea gripped the lead rope, but she was standing to Spirit's right.

"You lead a horse from the left," Cindy said gently. "You do most things with horses from the left: leading, saddling, and mounting. Spirit won't mind if you do things from the right, but some horses might."

Chelsea flushed. "I did know that. I just forgot."

Cindy tacked Ruling Spirit up in the barn and led him to a mounting block. Chelsea climbed quickly into the saddle and picked up the reins. "Now what?" she said.

"Let's take him around the stable yard." White-brook didn't have an indoor or outdoor ring. Cindy doubted if it would be a good idea to take even as gentle an ex-racehorse as Spirit out on the training track.

Chelsea sat up straight as Cindy led Spirit around the stable yard. "Am I doing okay?" she asked anxiously. "I've only ridden . . . well, just three times before. Twice on ponies at the county fair, and once on a horse at Melissa's."

"You're doing great." Chelsea's hand and leg positions weren't quite correct, but Cindy thought she seemed at ease in the saddle. "You look like you've had more experience than that riding."

Chelsea flushed with pleasure. "I read horse books all the time," she said. "Every single one I can get."

Spirit was only walking, but Cindy could see how thrilled Chelsea was with her ride. The little girl sat deep in the saddle, relaxing her shoulders and smiling. Cindy thought she could trust her out of the stable yard.

"Do you want to go out on the trails for a few minutes?" she asked.

Chelsea looked thoughtful. "I guess I like just staying here and getting a riding lesson. I mean, if I had a horse, I'd do both every day. . . . But I don't think I'll ever have my own horse."

"I bet you will someday, since your father's a trainer," Cindy said.

"I sure hope so." Chelsea sighed. "Sometimes I think I'll die if I don't get a horse!"

For the next hour Cindy coached Chelsea on her seat, hands, and cues. She could see the younger girl trying to put it all together. At the end of the hour Cindy was satisfied that Chelsea had made real progress.

"You still tend to jerk up your hands when you lose your balance," Cindy said. "Then your heels come up, too, and you *really* lose your balance. I'm not being critical—I'm just suggesting some things you could work on."

"I want to, but I don't know when I'll ride again." Chelsea shook her head.

"You can come over here sometimes." Cindy knew that she was already stretched pretty thin for time, with chores and schoolwork. But there was something compelling about Chelsea. And the younger girl was such a quick student, Cindy doubted if she'd have to babysit her on the horses for long.

Chelsea stared at Cindy, as if she couldn't believe her ears. Then her face lit up. "I could really ride again? Wow! Thanks so much!"

"I enjoyed it, too." Cindy saw the Billings' car coming up the driveway. "There's your mom," she said. "Let's put up Spirit."

"Okay." Chelsea correctly dismounted to the left. In the barn she helped Cindy put away Spirit's tack and brush him down. Cindy was pleased to see that

Chelsea seemed to enjoy caring for Spirit as much as riding him.

I should work with Honor, Cindy thought as she waved good-bye to the Billings. The early winter darkness was falling, and Cindy was even more tired from walking and trotting Chelsea around than she had been that morning. But Cindy hadn't been able to spend time with her favorite filly for days.

I can get in about half an hour with her, Cindy thought as she walked back to the paddocks. In the fading light she could barely see the nine yearling fillies in the side paddock. But Cindy had no trouble picking out Honor. The bright bay filly's coat gleamed, and Cindy could make out her imperious walk. Honor was circling the other fillies, as if she were rounding them up for dinner.

"Hey, Honor, are you bossing the other yearlings again?" Cindy called.

The bay filly's head jerked around, and she whinnied shrilly. The next second she was flying toward the gate, her long, graceful legs eating up the ground. The other fillies pounded behind her.

Honor stopped abruptly at the fence line and thrust her muzzle into Cindy's hands. "It's not quite dinnertime yet," Cindy said, rubbing the filly's black muzzle and star. *Honor is about as close to perfect in looks as a horse can get,* Cindy thought. Honor wasn't tall, but all the loveliness of Wonder's line had come through in her wide-set dark eyes and exquisitely sculpted head. Her conformation was flawless, from the correct slope of her shoulders and pasterns to the noble arch of her neck.

"Let's do a little work, then I'll take you in for dinner." Carefully Cindy reached down along one of the filly's front legs until she reached her hoof. After a moment's hesitation Honor let her pick it up. Cindy worked her way around all of Honor's hooves, then led her around the paddock.

The other fillies followed jealously, bumping each other and sometimes Cindy and Honor. Honor whirled at an especially hard nudge from Fleet Street and laid back her ears. Fleet Street jumped away.

"Honor, it's all right," Cindy said quickly. "She's not going to hurt you—she just wants attention, too." Honor's ears flicked at Cindy, then stayed back up. She continued to walk after Cindy. *Good*, Cindy thought. *She doesn't hold a grudge and lose her concentration—I don't need another Champion right now!*

Cindy and Honor continued around the paddock. In the dark Cindy couldn't see the fillies, but she could feel their hot breath on her arms and hands. She loved being surrounded by the exquisite young horses. They kept her warm as night fell and the winter cold returned.

Cindy stopped Honor and looked her over. The filly's bay coat was thick, and her breath misted around her whiskers. She was already taller than Cindy. "It's not hard to imagine riding you," Cindy said. "Summer seems a long way off, but it's just a couple of months. Then we'll start breaking you to saddle. That will be the first big step in getting you ready for races the year after, when you're two."

With every passing day Cindy yearned more to be Honor's exercise rider—and someday ride her in races. Teaching Chelsea had made Cindy realize that she had learned a lot about horses over the previous few years. She had exercise ridden and helped train Glory and Champion, but under unusual circumstances. Cindy had found Glory, a runaway from cruel trainers, and convinced everyone at Whitebrook first that he had talent, then to buy him. Champion's training had come at a time when Ashleigh was busy with other horses.

Cindy knew Ashleigh might want to bring Honor along herself. Honor was the only offspring of Townsend Princess, Wonder's daughter.

Well, Fleet Street and Lucky Chance need an exercise rider and a jockey, too, Cindy said to herself, patting Honor's neck. Ashleigh had promised that Cindy would be riding one of the three fillies. But Ashleigh hasn't said anything more about it. Cindy wondered if Ashleigh had forgotten her promise.

"Let's start bringing them in," Len called from the training barn.

"Okay!" Cindy clipped a lead line to Honor's halter and cast a last look over the beautiful filly. "You're so special," she said. "I hope I'm special enough to ride you."

8

"AND THEY'RE OFF!" THE ANNOUNCER SHOUTED AT THE start of the Florida Derby on March 16. "It's Wonder's Champion on the lead, showing good early speed and duplicating his performance in the Fountain of Youth. Back one to Secret Sign and Sky Beauty; Ruby's Slipper in third as they head into the first turn."

Go, Champion! Cindy willed the colt silently. She was smiling already. After his brilliant win in the Fountain of Youth, Champion was the most talked about three-year-old in the country. He was the even-money favorite in this race.

Cindy pushed back her damp hair, watching Champion closely. The day was hot, with clear Florida sunshine and a dry, fast track. The conditions were perfect for Champion to run.

Champion plunged into the backstretch, his almost black tail streaming out behind him. Secret Sign and Sky Beauty still closely trailed him. The other seven horses in the crowded field were bunched right behind the frontrunners. A solid ball of energy, the ten Thoroughbreds blazed into the far turn.

All those other horses will fall back, Cindy told herself confidently. *The horses in Champion's races always do.*

Almost immediately Secret Sign dropped back to fourth, then fifth. "Is Secret Sign out of the race, Dad?" Cindy asked hopefully. The gray colt was Champion's main competition.

"No, I don't think so—his jockey's just rating him," Ian replied.

Mike looked through his binoculars. "Champion's just where we want him. But he's setting fast fractions to stay ahead of Sky Beauty and the rest of the field."

"What a mob out there!" Samantha said nervously. "Ashleigh's bound to have traffic problems."

"There are a lot of strong contenders, too." Mike's tone was clipped.

"Like Champion." Beth leaned around Mike to smile at Cindy.

Cindy smiled back. But now that the horses were strung out along the backstretch, she could see that Sky Beauty was rapidly eating into Champion's lead. Cindy knew that the bay filly was a tough contender.

"It's Wonder's Champion by one as they head into the stretch," the announcer called. "But Sky Beauty is moving up to challenge!"

Cindy twisted her program with worry. "Champion can always go into his superdrive, can't he, Dad? Then he'll beat her."

"Maybe." Ian was gripping the rail tightly. "Sky Beauty seems to have a lot left."

With a sudden burst of speed Sky Beauty put her nose in front of Champion's. She was gaining with every stride, with just a furlong to the wire!

"No! Catch her, Champion!" Cindy cried. "Tell him, Ashleigh!"

As if she had heard, Ashleigh crouched flat over Champion's neck, asking the big colt for everything he had. In an instant Champion's strides became longer. He began to close the gap to Sky Beauty. "He has more," Cindy cried. "He's ahead of her!"

"But here comes Secret Sign to close," Mike shouted.

Cindy tore her gaze from Champion and Sky Beauty. To her horror, she saw that Secret Sign was closing like a bullet on the frontrunners. He had put away the three and four horses and was galloping after Sky Beauty.

Champion and Sky Beauty were running almost neck and neck directly in front of Secret Sign. "He can't get through," Cindy cried. "Champion will win it!"

"Shawn thinks he has to try!" Mike shouted.

Events were happening so fast that they blurred for Cindy. Secret Sign moved slowly but surely between Champion and Sky Beauty's flanks. Cindy half stood, silently begging Champion to do more. Champion's front legs were stretching for the wire, but Secret Sign was going to snatch his victory!

Champion seemed to be thinking the same thing. He turned his head toward the other colt and pinned his ears.

No! Cindy just had time to gasp. Champion bore out from the rail, and the two colts bumped with a sickening jolt. In that second Sky Beauty drew ahead of Champion.

Cindy almost screamed as Ashleigh and Shawn fought for balance. "Steady, Ashleigh!" Mike cried. His face was drawn with worry.

Ashleigh regained control almost immediately. She was up over Champion's neck, urging him on with all her might. Scanning the track frantically, Cindy realized that Champion was running with perfect, even strides. He hadn't hurt himself in the collision. Secret Sign had also recovered his stride.

"Ashleigh's got Champion straight again!" Mike shouted.

"But she's out of time!" Ian rubbed his forehead.

Sky Beauty swept under the finish line, a length ahead of the battling colts.

Cindy sank into her seat, clutching her ripped program. It barely registered that Champion had hung on for second place. *That was so scary when Champion and Ashleigh almost went down,* she thought. Looking at the concerned faces of her family, Cindy could see they felt the same way.

"Well, let's go talk to Ashleigh." Mike blew out a deep breath. His face was pale. Cindy knew that he must have feared for Ashleigh's life when the colts collided.

This is so different from the way I thought the day would turn out, Cindy thought unhappily as they hurried down to the winner's circle. *I shouldn't have been so sure Champion would win—no horse wins all his races.*

"Sky Beauty is a game filly," Ian said with a sigh. "Champion has to run his best to beat her."

"And he didn't." Cindy felt miserable. She'd thought Champion's problem of going after other horses was solved.

Ashleigh rode Champion over to the gap. The colt was lathered up and blowing. "He's really hot," Ashleigh said tersely. "Let's get him back to the barn and cooled out."

Cindy nodded, examining the colt closely. It was a hot day, but Champion didn't usually sweat much. She checked the board. The fractions from the race had been fast, but not killer. "He's so hot because he's upset," Cindy said.

"Probably," Ashleigh agreed as she dismounted.

Champion bumped Cindy hard with his head, letting her know that he wasn't calm yet. He had a quizzical, indignant expression, as if he couldn't believe he had lost. "Champion, you almost got hurt badly," Cindy said. She still felt a little dizzy from those terrible moments right before the wire. "Why did you rush at Secret Sign?"

Champion dropped his head. He seemed to be saying that he had no idea either. Cindy relented and rubbed his ears. The colt hadn't meant to put Ashleigh in danger.

"What happened out there?" Mike asked Ashleigh quietly. "Did Secret Sign interfere with Champion?"

"Yes, but Champion interfered even more with him." Ashleigh seemed deflated. "I already had a word with Shawn. We've both agreed that we have a problem, and it's not going to be solved by going to the stewards."

"Maybe we should try blinkers on Champion," Ian said.

"Maybe, if that would keep him from being distracted," Ashleigh agreed. "We had a pretty good shot until the last couple of seconds of the race."

"Why did Champion act like that?" Cindy shook her head. "He wants to win, doesn't he?"

Ashleigh glanced around. Several reporters were headed their way. "Cindy, let's take Champion to the backside and talk about it there," she said. "Ian and Mike can deal with the press—they're very good at it. I'm just not ready to talk about this with them right now."

"Okay." Cindy looked at Champion. His breathing was almost back to normal. The colt bumped her again with his nose, but more gently. He followed her calmly off the track.

"I don't know what you expect, boy, but I can't make Secret Sign disappear so you can win," Cindy said. She noticed that Secret Sign had disappeared for now—Shawn had taken him quickly off the track.

"No, but I think that is the problem," Ashleigh replied. "Champion has very strong likes and dislikes of people and horses. As he's gotten older, it's just been polarized. That's what worries me about this defeat, Cindy. We're seeing a pattern of bad behavior again in Champion's races."

"Champion can't want to lose," Cindy said as she and Ashleigh walked the colt in front of the shed rows to cool him out. "And I really think he wants to please us."

"Maybe he thinks he *is* doing what we want," Ashleigh said. "We do want him to win, and so he's trying to intimidate the other horses."

"Huh." *That makes more sense*, Cindy thought. She loved Champion, and she knew that he loved her. They both had faith in each other now, and the colt trusted Ashleigh, too.

"Well, in any case, I've got to keep Champion away from Secret Sign in the future," Ashleigh said. "But that's easier said than done. Secret Sign will almost certainly start in the Derby. But maybe the two colts will draw posts that are far apart."

Cindy was silent. She doubted if Ashleigh thought that was the answer, either.

"Champion's got to get over this." Ashleigh sounded frustrated. "Darn! He ran the next-to-last furlong of the race in eleven and four-fifths seconds— that's blindingly fast. I just know he has what it takes to win the Derby."

"I'm sure he does, too." Cindy ran her hand lovingly down Champion's neck. The colt seemed completely cool, but she wanted to give him an extra half hour of walking just to make sure. "What should we do?" she asked. Cindy saw her dad and Mike approaching across the stable yard.

Ashleigh frowned. "Well, we did have a contingency plan if Champion lost the Florida Derby." She looked at Mike.

"We'll race Champion in the Lexington Stakes at Keeneland," Mike said. "That's dropping him back to one and a sixteenth miles. Part of the problem today may have been that the race was a mile and an eighth. Champion never raced that far before."

Cindy winced. *Mike sounds like he's lost confidence in Champion*, she thought. Cindy hoped the problem wasn't that Champion couldn't handle the distance. The Kentucky Derby was a mile and a quarter, a full furlong longer than the Florida Derby had been. The competition would be even more fierce. Some Kentucky Derby contenders had followed the same warm-up route of races as Champion, but some were running at other tracks in the United States or in Europe. All of them would gather in Louisville for the Derby.

"When is the Lexington Stakes?" Cindy asked. "How long do we have to get him ready?"

"It's on April 21," Ashleigh said. She didn't look happy.

"But that's only two weeks before the Derby!" Cindy looked quickly at Ashleigh, shocked. "Won't that take a lot out of Champion?" she asked hesitantly. *Maybe too much*, she added to herself. What if Mike was right that Champion was having trouble with long races?

"Maybe it's a lot to ask of Champion." Ashleigh frowned. "But Cindy, it wouldn't be good to run him in the Kentucky Derby after such a poor finish today. We need to get him back up to form."

Cindy had to agree with that. *But how?* she thought as she circled Champion around the yard. The colt pushed her from behind with his nose, as if he was enjoying their familiar routine.

"Usually you understand what I want," Cindy said, running her hand along the colt's thick mane. "So listen. I want you to win, but I don't want you to do it by scaring the other horses. Being unsportsmanlike isn't the way to win. I thought you knew that."

Champion stopped dead. Either he was staring at a gray filly walking out of an adjacent shed row or he didn't care for her lecture.

The colt swung his head around to look at her, his dark eyes soft in his beautiful face. "Oh, I know," she said with a sigh. "I still love you, too. It's okay, boy."

She put her arms around his glossy brown neck and rubbed her cheek against his thick fur. "We'll get it together," she promised. "A horse as smart and talented as you just has to win the Derby."

9

TWO WEEKS LATER CINDY WOKE UP AND ROLLED OVER IN bed, trying to remember what was special about the day. The warm spring sun was streaming into her small, cozy room, almost bringing to life the flower print on her curtains and bedspread.

Cindy stretched lazily, enjoying the warmth on her face. *It's late—why did everyone let me sleep in?* she thought, putting her hands behind her head.

Suddenly she sat bolt upright. "It's my birthday! How could I forget that?"

Cindy quickly dressed in jeans and a T shirt and bounded down the stairs to the kitchen. *I guess it's no wonder I forgot about it*, she thought. Champion had returned to Whitebrook the day after his loss in the Florida Derby. From that moment on, Cindy had lived, eaten, and slept horses. She was determined to turn around the colt's loss so that he won in the Lexington, and after that the Kentucky Derby. Cindy didn't want to let the colt's Derby chance slip through her fingers if there was anything that she could do about it.

Beth and Samantha sat at the kitchen table, drinking coffee. Kevin was sitting quietly in his high chair, playing with spilled cereal on his tray.

"Happy birthday, Cindy," Beth said with a smile. "How does it feel to be fifteen?"

"Sweet fifteen and never been kissed," Samantha teased.

Cindy's face burned crimson. Max hadn't kissed her again since the night of the dance, but she had thought about that kiss a lot. She didn't know if he had, too. Cindy hadn't told anyone what had happened—it was much too private. But she wondered what her friends would think if she did tell them. "That's right, I've never been kissed," she stammered, putting her hands to her flaming cheeks.

"There'll be plenty of kisses in the future," Beth said hastily. "Cindy, your presents are in the living room. Do you want to open them now or wait until your party tonight?" Cindy had planned a big party. She'd invited all her friends in the ninth grade and Mandy.

"Are you kidding? I can't wait another second!" Cindy rushed into the living room, followed by

Samantha and Beth, carrying Kevin. A pile of brightly wrapped packages towered on the hearth.

Cindy tore into the wrapping paper. She got several new CDs from her parents and a gift certificate to her favorite tack store from Ashleigh and Mike.

"The CDs are just what I wanted, and so is the gift certificate," Cindy said, beaming. "I know just what I'm going to buy with the gift certificate—a leather halter for Honor Bright." The filly was so beautiful, she deserved better than an ordinary nylon halter, Cindy thought.

She held up a big square box. "This one's from Champion and Samantha," she said, reading the tag. She quickly opened the box. "A new riding helmet!" Cindy put it on her head. "Thanks, Sammy."

"You're welcome," Samantha said. "Champion and I knew you needed one."

I guess Champion did know, Cindy thought wryly. Her old helmet was pretty beat up, and Champion was the reason. The previous year he'd thrown her several times. The helmet hadn't survived the falls as well as Cindy had. She had also left it carelessly near Champion's stall one day, where she thought it was out of his reach. The colt had taken a couple of bites out of the cloth.

"I'm going down to the barn to thank Champion," she said.

Samantha nodded. "I'll be down in a little while. I already exercised Limitless this morning."

Cindy ran down the path to the barn, drawing

110

in deep breaths of cool air. The spring day was mild and still, and the trees in the stable yard were a soft, wispy green as their new leaves uncurled in the sunshine. *I won't have much time to exercise Champion this morning since I have school,* she thought. *I wish Mom and Sammy hadn't let me sleep in.*

Cindy had exercised the colt hard since his loss in the Florida Derby, preparing him for the Lexington Stakes in April. Champion had gone brilliantly for her, burning up the track in his works.

She grimaced. *Champion's works couldn't be better— except when Freedom and Vic get in his way,* she thought. That didn't happen often. Vic watched out for Champion and steered his mounts, particularly Freedom, away from him. Once when Vic had the bad luck to cross Champion's path with Freedom, Cindy understood what Ashleigh had meant when she said the colt's dislikes just got stronger. Champion had squealed with rage at Freedom and had run in place, trying to get at the other colt. Cindy had barely been able to hold him.

In the barn Champion was looking impatiently out of his stall, as if he knew she was thinking about him. The colt whinnied loudly and bobbed his head.

"I guess you can't wait to greet the day," Cindy said with a laugh.

Cindy's heart melted at the sight of the lovely colt. Champion might have had strong dislikes, but his loves were just as strong. Over the past two weeks

Cindy had felt her bond with the colt deepening even beyond what she had thought possible. Even though Champion was difficult, Cindy was more sure than ever that he was headed for great victories on the track.

"Just a minute, boy!" she called. Cindy glanced at the board in the office. Champion was scheduled only to walk that day, not to gallop or work. *I'd still better hurry, or I'll never make it to school on time,* Cindy thought. *Everybody should have their birthday off.*

A small shadow stalked Cindy as she walked toward Champion. Looking quickly around, Cindy saw her cat from the shelter trotting at her heels. "Are you coming with me to visit Champion, Kitcat?" she asked. Cindy hated to admit it, but she'd drawn a complete blank in naming the little tortoiseshell cat. She'd nicknamed her Kitcat while she tried to think of a better name, but so far none had come to mind. Cindy was troubled that Kitcat hadn't completely settled in at Whitebrook. She was still shy, even around Cindy, and she hadn't made friends with any of the other cats. Cindy was glad to see that the kitten was following her that day. That was a first.

Champion was restlessly stretching his head over the stall door. "We're going out, boy," she reassured him. She knew that Champion hated standing in his stall.

Cindy reached for the colt's tack, which Len had

thoughtfully laid on the half door of a vacant stall. She turned around just in time to see Kitcat jump up on Champion's back.

Cindy bit back a cry of alarm. Champion had never liked any cat at all, and she couldn't believe he would tolerate a cat on his back for a second. *If Kitcat starts to fall, the first thing she'll do is dig her claws into Champion*, Cindy thought. The high-strung colt was perfectly capable of shaking Kitcat off and slinging her into a wall, then trampling her.

Champion shuddered at Kitcat's sudden impact, and the cat teetered on his back. Cindy walked quickly but calmly back to the stall. She knew that if she yelled or hurried, it would only upset both animals more. She tried to reach over the stall door for the cat, but Champion was standing too far away.

The small cat righted herself and purred. *Maybe Champion can't feel her claws.* He had such a dense, carpet-like coat. "Come here, girl," Cindy said softly. But the cat only purred louder. Then she began to pace on Champion's back.

To Cindy's amazement, Champion did nothing. The colt's ears were at a relaxed angle, and he stood on three legs. He seemed to be thoroughly enjoying the cat's company.

This is some kind of miracle, Cindy realized. *Champion's never liked another animal so much before.*

The kitten sat down on Champion's back and began washing her paws. "I think I know just what to call you, little cat," Cindy said. "Best Pal."

Cindy stepped into Champion's stall and closed the door. Propping her back against the wall, she slipped down it to the floor, kicking her boots deep into the straw. Cindy knew she should get going on Champion's walk. But first she wanted to think about Champion's problem with other racehorses. She and Ashleigh hadn't made a dent in it. Otherwise Champion was in great shape for the Lexington Stakes.

"What should I do?" Cindy muttered. "Maybe it's my fault you're like this, Champion. I've made such a pet out of you. If you weren't so attached to me, maybe you wouldn't dislike other people and animals so much."

Hearing his name, Champion wandered over to visit. Cindy noticed with amusement that he seemed to be walking carefully, so as not to interrupt his cat guest's bath.

"Glory and Pride are both spoiled, and they were great racehorses," she continued as Champion nuzzled her hands. "They just tried harder because they were loved so much. As usual you've got things backward, Champion."

The colt tossed his head, looking pleased with himself.

"Here comes Imp," Cindy said. Glory's gray cat friend was also fond of Cindy, and he had hopped on the half door, ready to launch at Cindy. "Don't be nasty, Champion—"

The colt had already flattened his ears. Imp hissed

with alarm, but he jumped into the stall anyway. The dappled cat marched resolutely over to Cindy and walked onto her lap. Cindy ran her hand down the cat's back, keeping an eye on Champion. Imp arched his back and purred. Champion's ears went back up.

"Do you mean it?" Cindy asked Champion. "Or are you going to go after Imp the minute I have my back turned?"

Cindy set Imp on the straw next to Champion, careful to leave him where she could grab him back if Champion got excited. The colt bent his head to sniff Imp. Imp froze, and Cindy held her breath.

But the big colt merely nudged the cat. "Let's not push it, guys," Cindy said, slowly reaching for Imp. But before she could gather him up, Imp had twined himself around Champion's leg, purring. Champion stood relaxed, as if he liked nothing better in the world.

Why is Champion okay about Imp all of a sudden? Cindy wondered, looking from the cat to the colt. *What is going on here? All of a sudden he likes Best Pal and Imp, too. . . .*

"I know what it is!" Cindy stood up slowly, even in her excitement careful not to disturb the three animals. "You just realized I like Best Pal and Imp, Champion," she said. "Now you know they're okay. So all Ashleigh and I have to do for you to get along with the other racehorses is introduce you to them and show you that we like them. . . ."

Cindy slumped back down in the straw. "That sounds completely nuts," she muttered. Ashleigh, Mike, and Ian would never go along with a plan like that.

Cindy smiled as she pictured herself at the races, saying to trainers, owners, and jockeys, *Hi, I'm Cindy. Can my horse get to know your horse?*

"I guess that would be pretty silly," she said aloud. "But I know what I could do, Champion. I can give you a crash course in getting along with other horses right here at Whitebrook. Then when you meet up in races with Secret Sign and other horses you don't like, maybe it won't be such a problem."

Cindy frowned. She knew it was a big jump from Champion's getting along with a couple of cats at Whitebrook to tolerating a racehorse trying run to him off on the track at forty miles per hour. "I have to try something, don't I, boy?" she asked. "But first I have to sell Ashleigh on the idea."

Cindy carefully removed Best Pal from Champion's back and tacked up the colt. She was just about out of time before the school bus came, but she had to talk to Ashleigh about Champion. That wouldn't leave her any time to walk him, so someone else would have to take him around. Champion wouldn't like that unless it was Ashleigh, and Cindy hated to shirk her chores. *Maybe Mom and Dad will let me be late for school for once,* she thought as she led Champion down the aisle. *After all, it's my birthday!*

Cindy found her dad and Ashleigh in the stable office. Spring was a busy time at the farm, and she knew that both of them had been at work since before sunrise.

"I'm sorry to bother you," she said hesitantly. "But I had an idea about how to help Champion get along with other horses."

Ashleigh lifted her fingers from her computer keyboard and looked at Cindy. "What's that?" she asked.

Cindy tried to think how best to describe her plan. It had sounded strange even when she described it to herself. "Champion made a new friend this morning," she said.

Ian laughed. "How nice for him. Sorry, honey—I'm listening."

Champion fidgeted and pulled back on the reins. He seemed to be wishing Cindy would get to the point, too, so that they could go out.

Cindy frowned and started over. At least Ashleigh seemed to be taking her seriously. "You know Champion doesn't like cats," she said.

"That's true," Ashleigh replied. "I've noticed that."

"But he does now—he likes Imp, and he and Best Pal seem to adore each other," Cindy continued.

"Who's Best Pal?" Ian asked, smiling.

"My new cat." Cindy drew a deep breath and continued. She had to make her dad and Ashleigh understand. "All of a sudden Champion decided to like both cats because he saw that I do. I mean, I think he likes Best Pal naturally—they really hit it off this morning. But he only likes Imp because he saw me petting him."

"Honey, this sounds a little goofy," Ian said. "I don't mean to offend you, but what does all that have to do with racing Champion?"

Cindy faltered a little. "Well, I thought I could try to make Champion be friends with Freedom. I know we probably can't introduce Champion to all the horses in the field at a race. But maybe if he's getting along with the horses here, he won't go after horses at the track. He'll understand we don't want him to do that." Cindy looked pleadingly at her dad and Ashleigh. She really hoped they would agree that her plan had at least some merit. If they didn't, she didn't know what she'd do about Champion.

Ian looked skeptical. "I think Champion goes after other horses in his races because they're in his way and he's very competitive, not because he dislikes them."

Ashleigh nodded, and Cindy's heart sank. But then Ashleigh said, "I think you should try it, Cindy. We'll have to be very careful, though. This could backfire, and Champion might get even more solidified in his dislikes."

Cindy hadn't thought of that. "I'll go slow," she said. "I could start right now with Freedom."

"Do it tomorrow," Ian said firmly. "Ashleigh will walk Champion. You can't miss school."

"Just today . . ." Cindy begged.

Her dad shook his head. "Cindy, every single day

there's something you want to do with the horses that's important—so important, you just have to miss school. The answer is no. You've got seven minutes before the school bus leaves."

"Oh, all right," Cindy said with a heavy sigh. She had known that was what her dad's answer would be, but she thought it wouldn't hurt to make him feel a little guilty about it.

Ashleigh smiled at Cindy. "I did want to ask you one thing before you go."

"What?" Cindy asked eagerly. She could tell from Ashleigh's voice that something good was on the way.

"Will you ride Honor Bright this summer?" Ashleigh said.

Cindy's heart raced joyfully. This was her dream come true. "I'd love to more than anything!"

"Good." Ashleigh gave a brisk nod. "That's settled, then. I'll ride Fleet Street, and Sammy will train Lucky Chance."

"Wow!" Cindy's mind was whirling. *I'll be able to ride Honor in races when she's two,* she thought. *We'll both be old enough then. I wonder what that will be like!*

Cindy could hardly believe her good luck. In a daze she walked out of the office.

"Oh, Cindy?" Ashleigh called.

Cindy ducked her head back in the office doorway. "Yes?"

"Happy birthday," Ashleigh said.

Cindy beamed. "It's the best ever, thanks to you."

10

VERY EARLY THE NEXT MORNING CINDY WALKED DOWN TO
the training barn. She had set her alarm ahead an
hour to give herself extra time with Champion. Ian
had scheduled Champion for a slow gallop, and
Cindy also wanted to try out her plan to make
Champion and Freedom friends.

*I may need a little extra time to persuade Vic to go
along with this*, she thought, brushing back strands of
blond hair that had escaped from her ponytail. Cindy
hadn't spoken to Vic yet about her plan, but she
doubted he would like it much. Champion disliked
Vic even more than Freedom.

*I just have to make Vic realize that today will be differ-
ent*, Cindy said to herself, looking up at the sky. The
day was cloudy, with a bitter, damp wind. On days
like this, spring seemed to disappear back into winter.

120

But today might be an all right day for my experiment with Champion, she realized. He wasn't particular about the weather, as long as the track wasn't muddy. After intensive training the colt could handle a muddy surface, but it wasn't his favorite.

Cindy broke into a run, partly to beat the rain and partly because she could hardly wait to try out her plan on Champion. *I'm in such a great mood.* Her birthday party the night before had been fantastic. Cindy had gotten even more CDs from her friends, and now she had the latest CD of just about every hot group in the country. Heather had given her a video about training jumpers. Cindy was looking forward to watching the video and learning more about a different horse sport.

Not that I'm going to train jumpers, she thought as she headed down the aisle for Champion's stall. *I've got my hands full with just one Thoroughbred!*

Champion was waiting in his stall for her. The dark brown colt's thick forelock fell almost into his eyes as he pranced impatiently in place.

"You're full of yourself this morning," Cindy said with a smile, running her hand through his luxurious mane. "You might not be a big star yet, but you sure act like one." Cindy's party had moved down to Champion's stall, and all Cindy's friends had petted and admired the beautiful colt. Champion had soaked up all the attention and asked for more.

Len pushed a wheelbarrow by the stall. "Morning, Cindy," he said.

"Morning, Len." Cindy clipped a lead line to Champion's halter. "Do you know where Vic is?"

"He's already out with Freedom," Len replied.

Cindy nodded. "Good. I need to see both of them."

"Ashleigh told me about your idea for Champion," Len said. The older man winked. "I think you've got something there—horses are a lot smarter and more sensitive than most people give them credit for. Good luck."

"Thanks." Cindy was grateful for the support. She knew her dad was still skeptical about her idea. Ashleigh seemed neutral.

"Do you need help?" Len asked.

"Yeah, I think I do," Cindy said hesitantly. After her birthday party she had lain awake in bed, thinking out her plan for Champion. The plan seemed to her a good one, but she wasn't sure what might go wrong. Len's steadying presence would almost certainly help.

"I'll meet you at the track in five minutes," Len said, continuing down the aisle.

"Thanks." Cindy quickly tacked up Champion and led him out of the barn. The clouds had become even lower, turning into a fine mist sweeping the track. Cindy couldn't even see the far side of it.

Ian, Mike, and Ashleigh were already at the rail. Many of the horses in training were exercising as they prepared for the spring meets.

Suddenly Samantha burst out of the mist, breezing Limitless Time. Cindy stopped Champion for just a

122

second to watch the bay colt fly across the track, his breath coming in quick snorts and his hooves thundering on the damp track. Limitless Time flashed by the gap. "Wow, he looks good!" Cindy called. She thought the colt had definitely improved since his slow start as a two-year-old.

At the sound of Cindy's voice, Ian and Mike turned and smiled. *They think I'm crazy,* Cindy realized. *Maybe I am, but I'm going to try this anyway!*

Vic popped out of the mist on Freedom, trotting the colt. "Hey, Vic!" Cindy called.

Vic slowed the black colt at the gap. "What's up, Cindy?" he asked.

"I need your help with an experiment," Cindy said.

"If it involves him, I'm not sure I'm interested." Vic pointed to Champion.

Cindy looked at the colt. Champion's ears were already back a fraction, even though Freedom was twenty yards away.

Cindy could feel her heart sinking, but she didn't want to give up yet. She saw Len approaching from the training barn, so at least she'd have one supporter. "Please, Vic," she begged. "I want to try to get Champion over his dislike of Freedom. I really need you to help me. If we don't get Champion over his problems, we can kiss the Kentucky Derby good-bye. And maybe Champion's whole racing career, because if he keeps going after other horses, somebody's going to get hurt."

123

"Okay, okay." Vic relented. "You know I want Champion to start in the Derby as much as anyone. Just don't get Freedom or me killed. What do you want me to do?"

"I want to try two things," Cindy said. She had carefully thought this out the night before. "Would you mind getting off Freedom for a minute?"

Vic dismounted, and Cindy handed Champion's reins to Len. Then she gathered Freedom's reins and mounted up.

"Where are you going?" Vic asked. He didn't sound happy.

"Just around in a little circle." For five minutes Cindy walked and trotted Freedom in a circle, staying where Champion could see her. The well-trained black colt calmly followed the commands of his new rider.

Cindy dismounted and leaned against Freedom's shoulder. Then she rubbed both sides of her hands along the colt's neck and walked back to Champion, handing Freedom's reins to Vic. "Okay, Champion," she said. "Take a good sniff."

The colt dropped his elegant head and pricked his ears. Cindy let him thoroughly sniff her hands, then rubbed his neck. Champion didn't react at all to Freedom's scent. "Now we try part two," she said.

"What's that?" Vic asked warily.

"We're going to get these two used to each other in person."

Vic groaned. "Be really careful, Cindy! I don't want my colt anywhere near that demon."

"What are you going to do, Cindy?" Len asked calmly.

"The same thing we would if Champion was spooking from an object—we'll lead them closer together, very slowly, until Champion realizes that it's okay. How does that sound?" Cindy looked hopefully at Len.

Len nodded. "Let's try it. I'll hold Champion, and you take Freedom."

Cindy turned to Vic. "Do you mind if I hold Freedom? Champion might not be able to handle getting over his dislike for Freedom and you in one day."

"Suits me fine," Vic muttered, stepping to the side.

"The lesson's simple since this isn't a race," Len said quietly.

"That's true." For a moment Cindy felt her confidence slipping again. *But I know how Champion thinks*, she assured herself. *This probably wouldn't work for any other horse. It may not work with him, either, but I've got a shot.*

"Just a few steps at a time," Len instructed. "Stop if either colt acts upset."

Cindy walked forward slowly with Freedom. He came willingly a few paces, and so did Champion. "So far, so good," Cindy called.

"Closer," Len answered.

Cindy moved Freedom out again. This time he was reluctant. He and Champion were within about twenty feet of each other now, and the black colt clearly didn't want to go anywhere near Champion.

125

After another few steps Freedom balked, digging in his heels.

Cindy saw that Champion was getting upset, too, but he wasn't slowing down. The big colt's ears were pinning closer to his head with every step. *He wants to get at Freedom!* she realized with alarm. *I hope Len can hang on to him.*

"Cindy, this isn't working and it never will," Vic protested urgently. "Besides, it's starting to rain."

"Wait just a second—" Cindy begged. Her words were cut short as Champion lunged at Freedom. Len quickly pulled the colt's head around, circling him. Cindy backed Freedom up several paces.

"That was close," Vic said shakily.

"Maybe we should stop," Len said. "Both colts are getting upset. And Champion still has to get in a gallop this morning."

The colt's behavior had frightened Cindy, too, and she did want to take Champion for his gallop. But she was sure that what they were doing was just as important as exercise—maybe even more critical.

"Let's try just once more," she said. "I'll do something different—I'll stand in front of Freedom instead of to his side. Champion might like that better."

"That horse doesn't like anything but intimidating other horses," Vic said.

Cindy ignored this comment. She stepped in front of Freedom and determinedly led the black colt toward Champion.

"Cindy, be careful," Len said quietly. "You're putting yourself at risk."

"Champion won't hurt me." Cindy knew that Len was worried Champion might run her down trying to reach Freedom, but she was sure Champion would never do that.

She and Len led the two colts within a few paces of each other. Champion craned his neck to reach Cindy.

"See? It's all right, boy," she said, rubbing his nose, then Freedom's nose. Champion's ears pricked, then one ear stayed up and the other tilted back. Cindy could almost see the colt making up his mind. At last both ears tipped into a relaxed position.

"Yes! We did it." Cindy cautiously stepped forward to rub Champion's neck.

"Good job." Len nodded approvingly.

Cindy heard a cheer go up from Ashleigh, Ian, and Mike. She had been so absorbed in the horses, she had forgotten the three trainers were there. "Way to go, Cindy!" Ashleigh called.

"I didn't enjoy that." Vic shook his head.

"Thanks so much for helping, Vic," Cindy said. She knew it couldn't have been easy for him to risk his favorite colt.

"You're welcome." Vic sighed. "Even though I know that tomorrow you're probably going to start on *my* part of the lesson."

"Maybe!" Cindy grinned and swiftly mounted up on Champion. "Let's go, boy," she said. "Are you ready for your gallop? We have to hurry before the rain gets any worse."

The fresh droplets stung Cindy's face as she trotted the colt counterclockwise around the track. Champion's wet coat was a gleaming black, and the drifting, charcoal-colored clouds made the day seem very dark.

Champion slipped a little on the muddy surface, and Cindy caught her breath. "Careful, boy," she said.

The colt recovered his balance and trotted on, shaking raindrops from his mane. Cindy relaxed.

We'll do the exact same thing with Freedom tomorrow, just to make sure Champion got the message, she thought. *Then I'll gallop them together.* "So far, the plan's worked perfectly," she said aloud. "Now we just have to see what happens in a race."

11

JUST BEFORE POST TIME ON APRIL 21, THE DAY OF THE Lexington Stakes, Cindy ran a finishing cloth over Champion's thick, smooth dark coat. *I'm glad Champion's last race before the Kentucky Derby is close to home,* she thought. Champion had been moved to the Keeneland track three days earlier, but Cindy had been able to visit him every day without missing school.

Champion turned in the crossties to nudge her affectionately. "You don't seem as keyed up as you usually are on race day," she said, patting his nose. Cindy hoped the extra attention she'd given the colt over the past few days had helped to make him happier and more relaxed. "I think it's good for both of us when I see you a lot," she said.

Champion bobbed his head vigorously, as if he entirely agreed.

129

Len walked down the stable aisle, carrying a lead line. "Is our Champion ready?" he asked with a wink.

"Almost." Cindy smiled back, but she felt the usual pre-race butterflies start in her stomach.

The field for this race is challenging, but Champion should be able to handle it, she reminded herself as she rubbed the last few inches of Champion's shoulder to a high gloss. *I really think we've got Champion over his problems with other horses.*

Over the previous few weeks Cindy had exercised Champion often with Freedom and other Whitebrook horses. The first time with Freedom had been nerve racking. But Champion had behaved perfectly, even when Freedom crowded him a little against the rail.

The Lexington Stakes was a good comeback race for Champion. That year most of the Derby contenders had bypassed it, including Sky Beauty and Secret Sign. Cindy hoped that meant Champion would have an easier race. She was still worried about running him so close to the Derby.

Cindy dropped her finishing cloth into Champion's tack trunk. "Okay," she said to Len. "I'm done."

"He looks set." Len patted Champion's neck and unclipped the crossties.

"Doesn't he?" Cindy admired the colt as Len led him out of the shed row. The late spring day was sunny and warm, and the branches of the big trees at the track were waterfalls of new, light green leaves. Cindy couldn't imagine a better day to be at the races.

Champion craned his neck to look at the other horses on the backside, pricking his ears and snorting a little. The colt's brisk, energetic walk told Cindy that he knew he was about to race and wanted nothing more.

That's good, she thought. *This race is important.* If Champion didn't win, Cindy doubted if Mike, Ian, and Ashleigh would run him in the Derby.

Champion stood quietly in the saddling paddock while Len tacked him up. Then Len and Ian took Champion around with the rest of the field. Cindy joined Ashleigh and Mike, who were standing at the far end of the walking ring.

"What do you think of the competition?" Cindy asked Ashleigh.

Ashleigh narrowed her hazel eyes thoughtfully. "It's a field of six—not too big, so maybe I won't have horrendous traffic problems. But some good horses will be out there. Sunshine Kiss and Monday Morning both won stakes at Santa Anita this winter. They may be Derby contenders if they pull an upset today."

Cindy knew who the upset would be over. Despite Champion's loss in the Florida Derby, he was going into the Lexington as the odds-on favorite.

Cindy saw a frown flit across Ashleigh's face. "What's the matter?" she asked.

"Nothing much." Ashleigh gave a half smile. "I definitely hesitate to run Champion so soon before the Derby. But I want to get a win under our belt."

"Duke's Devil looks good," Cindy commented. The black colt was on the opposite side of the walking ring from Champion, calmly following his handler. "I don't think Champion will bother him, do you?"

"I don't know, Cindy. We're expecting a lot out of Champion." Ashleigh shook her head. "He's a smart horse, but he is just a horse. I don't know if we can expect him to understand that since he gets along with Freedom, his old enemy, he's not supposed to bother other horses."

I think Champion is that smart, but I don't know if I can prove it today, Cindy thought. Champion seemed to be over his dislike of Duke's Devil—he hadn't bothered him in the Fountain of Youth. "I guess we'll find out when Champion runs against Secret Sign," she said.

"Secret Sign will be running in the Derby unless he's injured," Mike remarked.

"I know." Cindy was already wondering what she could do to better the chances that Champion would get along with Secret Sign at Churchill Downs. She was sure Champion would remember his dislike for the other colt—Champion had an extremely long memory.

"Here comes our boy," Ashleigh said affectionately as Len and Ian brought over the colt.

Champion whinnied a little in response. Other than herself, Cindy knew that Ashleigh was his favorite person.

The young jockey sprang into the saddle with a hand from Mike. Cindy briskly rubbed Champion's shoulder. "You know what you have to do, boy," she said. "No monkey business."

Champion dropped his head into her hands and sighed heavily, as if he could hardly believe what he was hearing. Then he jerked his head up with a snort.

"Okay, I'm going to get out there." Ashleigh touched her crop to her helmet. "See you in a bit."

"Watch him," Mike cautioned. "He's going to be next to Duke's Devil in the gate."

Ashleigh gathered her reins. "Got it."

In the stands Cindy watched the post parade impatiently. She was anxious for the race to be off. For once the post parade, where spectators had a last chance to view the horses, wouldn't tell her much about how the race would go. Most of the horses in the field for the Lexington were from the West Coast, and Cindy wasn't familiar with their running styles. She had heard that Sunshine Kiss, a chestnut colt, had closed strongly to win his last race at Santa Anita. But she would just have to watch and see how the rest of the horses did.

"Since the Lexington Stakes is only one and a sixteenth miles, that's less time for Champion to get into trouble," Mike said. "If he's planning any."

Cindy frowned. *The Kentucky Derby is a mile and a quarter,* she thought. *It sounds like Mike is still worried that Champion can't handle that distance.*

Beth looked at Cindy with her eyebrows raised. Cindy could see that she was wondering the same thing.

Probably Champion's performance that day would make up Ian and Mike's minds about the Derby. Cindy leaned forward, praying the colt would give the race his all and not have bad luck.

The horses loaded in the gate. Cindy was pleased to see that Champion left Duke's Devil alone, even though both horses loaded first into the one and two slots.

"I guess I'm glad Duke's Devil is here," Cindy said to Samantha. "If Champion doesn't bother him again, maybe he'll leave Secret Sign alone in the Derby."

"I sure hope Champion's over that problem," Samantha said quietly.

"Me too." Cindy looked back at the track. *Champion really needs a victory here,* she realized.

"The horses are in the gate," the announcer called. Cindy held her breath, watching the six colts shuffle in the narrow gate slots. Seconds later the bell clanged into the silence. Six determined Thoroughbreds lunged out of the gate, their deep-digging hooves throwing up an instant wall of dust.

"Champion broke well," Ian said excitedly. "There he goes to the lead!"

"Great—now he won't be trapped behind horses." Cindy watched tensely through her binoculars as the field rounded the clubhouse turn. She knew that

Champion would have to keep the lead a long way. The horses had to completely circle the mile-and-a-sixteenth-long track. The closers wouldn't make their move until near the end of the race.

"It's Wonder's Champion on the lead; back a length to Sunshine Kiss; Monday Morning is in third and Star Crossed in fourth; Night Watch is fifth, running in between horses; and Duke's Devil trails the field," the announcer called.

The horses rushed into the backstretch. Slowly but steadily Champion increased his lead over Sunshine Kiss to two lengths. "Did Ashleigh let him out or did he do that on his own?" Mike shouted over the swelling noise of the crowd.

"Either way, it was a good move," Samantha said.

Cindy relaxed just a fraction. Champion was running well, his strides perfect and regular. All he had to do was keep it up until the wire.

"Champion's the only speed in the race," Ian said. "And the track's been favoring speed today."

"Duke's Devil has that powerful closing kick," Mike commented.

"But Champion beat him in the Fountain of Youth anyway!" Cindy quickly focused her binoculars. Champion swept into the far turn, still on the lead by two lengths.

"Now we'll see what the closers do," Ian said. His voice was calm, but Cindy saw his jaw tighten.

At the three-eighths pole Sunshine Kiss, Monday Morning, and Duke's Devil began to move up on

Champion, running three abreast. They were all out to get the lead!

Cindy gripped Beth's hand. "Hang on, Champion!" she cried. "Please!"

The dark chestnut colt seemed to know exactly what to do. His strides flattened as he extended, reaching for unbelievable amounts of ground. Within seconds Champion had pulled away effortlessly. "That's it!" Cindy shouted, jumping to her feet. "Yes! Go for it, boy!"

"Wonder's Champion has plenty of run left," the announcer called. "He's ahead by four—he runs un-challenged to the wire!"

Champion galloped for the finish. His head was high, and his silken mane and tail flew out behind him as he swept through the final furlong.

"He's back," Cindy cried, torn between laughing and happy tears. "He won going away!"

Samantha hugged her. "This is wonderful!"

Cindy couldn't stop smiling as she walked down to the winner's circle. On the track the reporters were already mobbing Ashleigh. Champion was skit-tering around with excitement, his back end nearly bumping the spectators. Cindy quickly grabbed his reins.

The colt stopped fidgeting for a moment to touch his nose to her hands. Then he was off again, jerking his head repeatedly and bobbing on his front hooves. Soon Cindy's arms ached from trying to hold him still. "Oh, settle down," she scolded in a teasing voice. "You are one fantastic horse—you don't have to keep telling me."

"Look at him," Samantha said, laughing. "Don't you think he knows it?"

"I didn't really ask Champion for much today," Ashleigh was saying to the reporters. "He just did what he had to do—and, best of all, what he was told to do."

"He ran a clean, honest race," Ian agreed.

He sure did, Cindy thought proudly. *And now we can look ahead again!* A shiver coursed up her arms at the thought of Champion's next race. This victory cinched what it would be. In less than two weeks Champion would start in Thoroughbred racing's greatest challenge, the Kentucky Derby.

Three days before the Derby, Cindy stood nervously in the Kentucky Derby Museum, next to the Churchill Downs track, waiting for post positions to be drawn for the race. The room was crammed with trainers and owners, including Ashleigh, Mike, Ian, and Samantha.

"I wish they'd get started with the drawing," Heather whispered. "The suspense is killing me." Cindy had asked Heather to come with her to the drawing and then to a horses in training sale at the Sports Spectrum, a few miles down the road from the track.

"They're drawing the first number." Cindy watched as the racing secretary pulled a paper out of a box.

"Wonder's Champion!" he read. "Wow, Champion's

going to be assigned his position first!" Cindy said excitedly. Another racing official had drawn a wood number out of a bottle. "That'll be Champion's post position."

"Number one!" the man said.

"Cindy, can you believe it?" Samantha cried. "What a great position!"

Cindy grinned, relief flooding her. This year fourteen horses were starting in the Derby. The race was tough enough without a horse and jockey's trying to get through ten or twelve horses to reach the rail. As the drawing went on, she saw grimaces on the faces of several owners and trainers whose horses had drawn posts far to the outside.

"So can we go to the horse sale now?" Heather asked.

"Wait, I want to see what positions the rest of the field draw," Cindy said.

"Secret Sign—number three," the official said. Secret's Sign's trainer and owner exchanged smiles.

"Uh-oh." Cindy winced. That position was good for Secret Sign, but she had been hoping Champion and Secret Sign would start far away from each other. Instead they would be almost neighbors.

"That's the end of the drawing," Ashleigh said, joining the girls. "Let's go to the sale."

"Sounds good." Cindy looked carefully at Ashleigh to see how she felt about the post draw. Ashleigh seemed chipper. She didn't seem concerned about Secret Sign. But Cindy couldn't help worrying.

"Cheer up, Cindy—Champion drew a really good

post position, right?" Heather said as they walked to the car.

"I know." Cindy sighed. "It's hard not to wonder what Champion and Secret will do to each other in the race, though. But I guess I can't expect everything to be perfect."

"Well, try to forget about it for a little while," Heather said. "Be excited—we're going to a horse sale, and you might buy a horse!"

"Maybe." Cindy brightened at the thought. "We don't usually buy at this sale. Mike, Dad, and Ashleigh are just thinking that we might find a bargain—an inexpensive horse that they can train into a winner."

But as Ian drove over to the sale, Cindy could feel her excitement building. She wondered if they would buy a horse and, if so, what he would be like.

"Don't get your heart set on any of the horses, Cindy," Ian said as he pulled into the parking lot. "I've gone through the catalogue, and I'm going to look at a few of them. But we haven't decided to buy."

"I like sales where we're buying, not selling," Cindy said as they walked to the auction grounds. "I hate it when Whitebrook horses are sold."

"Unfortunately that's part of the horse business," Ashleigh remarked. "Otherwise Whitebrook would be so full of horses, we'd have to put them in the house."

Cindy smiled. "I know, I know."

Ashleigh smiled back. "That doesn't sound bad."

"Does it sound bad that Champion and Secret Sign are starting so close in the Derby?" Cindy asked.

Ashleigh shrugged. "It's the luck of the draw. I'm not looking at it as bad luck. I just have to deal with it."

"Maybe we need to let Champion and Secret Sign get to know each other before the race," Cindy said. *I bet Ashleigh won't go for that*, she thought.

Ashleigh shook her head. "Cindy, that's just not professional. Besides, how on earth could we do that with Champion before every race? We don't even know which horses he might take a dislike to. We'll just have to hope that he's learned the general lesson about leaving other horses alone—and that I can keep him in hand during the Derby."

Cindy nodded. She really couldn't argue with that. *But I think Champion has learned*, she consoled herself as they walked up to the first horse on Ian's list. A groom was just returning the colt to his stall after showing him to another potential buyer.

Cindy's gaze was riveted to the gorgeous black colt. His conformation looked perfect to her: correct legs, well angled at the pastern; a deep, powerful chest; and a perfectly sloped shoulder. His coat looked as soft and plush as black velvet. He had no markings other than a small star.

But Cindy was most impressed by the colt's expression. His eyes were as black as his coat, and they seemed soulful and sad.

"That's the blackest horse I ever saw," Heather whispered.

"He's just beautiful," Cindy murmured. "Why is he for sale here? I guess because he's older."

"All of these horses are older," Ian said. "They're age three and up, so I'm not going to find a Breeders' Cup Juvenile or Derby winner here. But you can tell more about older horses. Black Reason has raced, but he was sold when his owners discovered a bone chip in his knee. As far as I can tell, he's recovered fully after the arthroscopy done to remove it."

Cindy knew that arthroscopy was a medical procedure used on horses with bone injuries. An instrument that contained a camera was inserted through a small incision in the horse's skin. Guided by the camera, the veterinarian could remove pieces of bone with the instrument. Horses recovered more quickly than they would have if they'd had surgery.

"May we see him, please?" Ashleigh asked the groom.

The groom nodded. He walked the black horse up and down in front of the shed row.

Cindy looked carefully at the colt's legs. She couldn't see any sign of his injury, either on his skin or in the way he walked.

"Very nice," Ashleigh commented. "Thank you," she said to the groom.

"We'll see what he goes for," Ian said as they walked away.

Cindy looked back at Black Reason. The colt's gaze followed them. *He seems so sad*, she thought. *I can tell he's been in a lot of pain.* Her heart wrenched.

"If we buy you, I'll be so good to you," she promised.

Ian and Ashleigh looked at a few other horses, but Cindy wasn't nearly as impressed with them as she had been with Black Reason. One filly toed out slightly, and another colt had a swollen hock.

Cindy settled into her seat in the stands and looked around Samantha at Ian and Ashleigh. "So what did you think of Black Reason?" she asked.

"His pedigree is distinguished, at least on his father's side," Ashleigh commented.

"He may not have raced well because of the bone chip," Ian said.

It sounds like they want to buy him! Cindy and Heather exchanged hopeful looks.

As the first horses were led in front of the audience to be auctioned, Cindy wondered what it would be like to train an older horse again. Glory had also been three when she found him, but he had been terribly abused by earlier trainers. *Black Reason might have some bad habits,* she thought, *but he probably won't be afraid of the track or people, the way Glory was.*

"Here comes Black Reason," Heather said. The black colt was obediently following a handler.

Cindy sat up straight and glanced at her dad and Ashleigh. They were waiting calmly for the bidding to begin. Cindy knew they probably wouldn't jump in right away.

The black colt stood very still, staring out at the audience. "He's looking for you, Cindy." Heather giggled.

"Yeah, right." Bids on the black colt followed briskly. Cindy realized she wasn't the only person impressed with Black Reason's looks.

"And I have thirty thousand," the auctioneer said. "Who'll raise the bid to thirty-one?"

Ian lifted his program. "I have thirty-one thousand," the auctioneer continued. "Thirty-one thousand once . . ."

"You've got him!" Heather said. "Wow, Cindy!"

"The bidding's not over until the auctioneer bangs his gavel." But Cindy could feel her excitement growing, too.

"I have thirty-two thousand!" the auctioneer said suddenly.

Cindy and Heather stared at each other in dismay. Cindy looked quickly at her dad to see if he would bid again.

Ian frowned, then leaned over to consult with Ashleigh.

Please buy Black Reason, Cindy prayed. She was sure the black colt needed to come to Whitebrook. He seemed so sweet and sensitive, and so in need of a good home.

Ian lifted his program. "I have thirty-two thousand, five hundred," the auctioneer said.

"Yes!" Cindy whispered, sliding to the edge of her seat. Would the other buyer raise his bid?

"Going once, going twice . . . sold to buyer fifty-three," the auctioneer said.

"He's ours. We can go get him!" Cindy led the way

143

out of the stands. "This is great!" She was already planning to ask Ashleigh if she could ride him.

"We lucked out," Ashleigh said. "That was a Japanese buyer bidding against us—they can usually go high."

"There he is!" Cindy hurried over to the colt's stall. Black Reason was pacing nervously inside, occasionally stopping to look out the doorway. *He's upset because this is a strange place and he's surrounded by strange people,* Cindy thought sympathetically.

Black Reason caught sight of Cindy and nickered. "I remember you, too," Cindy said, going to the colt's head. "Everything's going to be just fine."

She helped Ashleigh hold the colt while Ian filled out paperwork. Black Reason sniffed Cindy's hands carefully. His ears were still pricked, but some of the tension was gone from his body.

"Yes, good things are going to happen to you now," Cindy said, gently stroking his neck. "I know some people think your racing days are over. But I think you're just getting started."

12

ON DERBY MORNING AT CHURCHILL DOWNS, CINDY walked backward to Whitebrook's shed row, surveying the colorful crowd. Superb Thoroughbreds were a dime a dozen at the track. Everywhere Cindy looked, gorgeous, gleaming black, brown, and gray horses followed their grooms and trainers. The people were just as sleek and well groomed as the horses. Many of the women wore wide brimmed, floppy hats and summery, silken long dresses. The men favored jackets and ties.

Cindy swallowed hard and reminded herself not to act like a little kid. But she wanted to jump for joy. She loved being part of this handsome, cheerful crowd.

The day was perfect, too—bright and sunny, but not hot. Cindy stretched her arms, basking in the warmth. "I think everyone has Derby fever," she said to Beth, who was carrying Kevin. The small boy squirmed, trying to get down. Christina was watching the race with her grandparents.

Beth smiled. "I sure do. Don't you feel like you're in a movie, Cindy? We've seen so many replays of the race on TV and video, it's hard to believe we're really here."

Cindy knew what Beth meant. Whitebrook hadn't had a Derby starter since the great days of Wonder's Pride, six years earlier. That had been before Cindy lived at Whitebrook. "It's good to be here," she said.

From Whitebrook's shed row Cindy heard a loud, familiar whinny. "Champion, what's gotten into you?" she asked, hurrying to the colt's stall. Today of all days she couldn't have him upset.

The dark brown colt dropped his head over the stall half door and leaned against it. He couldn't have made his wishes more clear: *I want out.*

"I was just about to let him graze," Len said, walking up to her. "He's been fidgeting and rolling since early this morning. The last thing we need is for him to get cast in his stall."

Cindy nodded, already reaching for a lead rope. She knew that sometimes horses rolled in their stalls and got stuck, unable to get up. They could injure themselves struggling. "You just want to go where the action is, don't you, boy?" she asked.

Champion bobbed his head vigorously, as if to say, *Finally someone understands.*

"It's going to be a long day," Len said with a smile.

"We've got to keep him occupied all morning and most of the afternoon until the Derby goes off."

Cindy smiled, feeling a delicious shiver spread all the way to her fingertips at Len's words. "I'll take care of Champion," she said. "I won't leave him at all. We'll have fun."

She stayed with the colt the whole day, not even taking a break to see the other races. Beth brought her lunch, but Cindy only poked at her hamburger. She was already too excited to eat.

"This is such a big day for you," she told Champion as she brushed him thoroughly for the third time that afternoon. "I don't know if you realize how big. Out of three hundred and sixty Triple Crown nominees, only fourteen are running—and you're one of them. That's still a big field, but it's a huge honor to be selected to run in the Derby at all."

Champion's ears flicked as he listened. He loved being brushed, and as Cindy's deep strokes relaxed him, the colt's eyes almost closed. The prospect of a Derby run didn't seem to be scaring him a bit.

An hour later Ashleigh walked into the shed row. "I'm going to change into my silks," she said. "It's almost post time."

Champion was repeatedly tossing his head and sidestepping. Suddenly he had woken up. "I think he knows what's coming," Cindy said.

"I think so, too." Ashleigh nodded. "That's good, because we need him on his toes. This is going to be a fiercely contested race. Sky Beauty is going in as the

147

favorite, then Champion and Secret Sign are tied for second choice."

Cindy's hands shook a little as she dropped her grooming tools in Champion's tack trunk. *Champion may fight with Secret Sign, but I'm sure he can outrun him,* she thought. *I'm more worried about Sky Beauty.* The powerful bay filly had won six out of her last eight races and had never placed off the board, or worse than third. And she had beaten Champion in the Florida Derby.

"Let's get him out to the saddling paddock," Len said.

Cindy gave a firm nod. This wasn't the time for an attack of nerves. "Okay, Champion," she said, unclipping him from the crossties. "This is it."

Champion tried to rush out of the barn, and Cindy had to pull on him hard to make him listen. "You'll be out there in a little while," she reassured him. *Champion loves to run,* she reminded herself. He just had to remember that was the important thing, not chasing other horses.

"Len, do you think Champion can beat Sky Beauty?" she asked as they walked the colt to the saddling paddock.

"I think so," Len replied. "Nancy Keegan, Sky Beauty's jockey, is a real pro, and she's taken advantage of the problems we've been having with Champion. But if our colt runs a clean race, I still think he can win."

Cindy looked back at Champion, floating behind her at an easy, graceful walk. From his small, well-shaped ears to the clean white of his satiny

148

white stockings, he was so beautiful, he made her heart ache. "Champion, I think you're going to win it today," she told him.

Ian met them in the saddling paddock. "Let's take him around, Len," he said. Cindy stepped back as the two men led Champion into the walking ring. Most of the horses had only one handler, but Cindy knew that after all the trouble they'd had last year with the colt in the walking ring, her dad felt better with backup.

Samantha joined Cindy, and together they watched the parade of exquisite horses in the walking ring. "Here comes Sky Beauty," Cindy murmured. The muscular bay filly was confidently walking after her handler.

"She's always tough," Samantha commented. "There's Ashleigh. Let's see if she has any last thoughts about the race."

Ian and Len brought Champion over to Ashleigh, and she quickly mounted up to get him out to the track. Cindy knew that part of Whitebrook's game plan for the Derby was to keep Champion away from other horses as much as possible.

"Take him straight to the lead if you can," Ian said. "That's where he likes to run, and it'll keep him out of trouble—we hope."

"Got it." Ashleigh gave Cindy a quick smile and turned Champion toward the tunnel. "This one's for Wonder," she said.

Cindy nodded, feeling a lump in her throat. She reached to stroke the colt's nose one last time. Champion had come so far to be here on this day. Cindy thought back to the contentious foal Champion had been. Talented but headstrong, he had tested her daily, but she had never lost faith in him. That faith was being rewarded today as the colt started in the Kentucky Derby. *No matter what happens, I'm proud of him*, she thought.

Champion bumped her lightly with his nose, as if to remind her that they were an unbeatable team.

Cindy blinked back tears. "Go get 'em, Champion," she said firmly. "By the end of the day Whitebrook will have three Derby winners."

"That's the spirit," Samantha agreed.

The colt marched toward the tunnel, his head held high. Sky Beauty followed him with Nancy Keegan up, and then Secret Sign and Shawn Biermont.

Nancy Keegan glanced at the Whitebrook group. Cindy knew that the dark-haired young jockey was starting to make a name for herself at the Churchill Downs track.

She's probably hoping we're going to have trouble with Champion again today and make her job easy, Cindy thought. *Well, we're not!*

In the post parade Ashleigh kept Champion well away from the other horses. Cindy knew that the field was an unusually good one, even for the Kentucky Derby. King Louie, a gray French horse, had won several big European races and a race at Gulfstream that winter. *So he shouldn't have a problem with American weather or tracks*, she thought. Greek Mystery, a smallish chestnut, had just shipped in

150

from California. He loved speed-favoring tracks, and the track at Churchill Downs had been favoring speed horses all day. The other Derby contenders were equally well qualified.

Champion's the best, Cindy told herself confidently as she walked to the stands. With his wins in the Bonus Series the previous year and his Fountain of Youth and Lexington Stakes victories, she was sure he belonged here every bit as much as the other horses.

Cindy sat down in the stands and looked out at the track. Champion jumped across the track a little and repeatedly asked for rein, but he seemed to be doing mostly what Ashleigh wanted. "So far he seems wired but not out of control," Cindy said.

"I hope Champion doesn't act up." Mike ran his hands through his blond hair. "In some ways he's the biggest long shot Whitebrook's ever entered in the Derby."

"They said that about Wonder, too," Ian said. "I remember the story well. But look how that Derby turned out."

"That's true," Mike agreed.

Cindy shot her dad a grateful look, then turned her attention to the track. Champion had just loaded in the one hole. He seemed to be waiting patiently for the other horses to join him. Ashleigh was rubbing his neck.

The other horses loaded easily. Cindy took a deep breath as the fourteen horse, the last horse in the field, was guided into the gate. *This is it*, she thought.

Cindy didn't want to miss the break from the gate,

but for just a second she took her eyes off the track and looked around. She wanted to remember every second of that special day. Cindy tried to memorize the way the sunshine lit up the infield, where thousands of people were partying, and how the flower-bedecked winner's circle looked. In minutes the Kentucky Derby winner would stand in that circle, accepting a blanket of red roses. Cindy looked back at the gate.

After a last second of tense silence the bell rang and the chutes flipped open, releasing the pent-up power of fourteen Thoroughbreds. The Kentucky Derby was off!

Champion broke cleanly from the gate. His strides big and quick, the colt roared into gear. But Sky Beauty's break was better, to Cindy's dismay. Sky Beauty's jockey immediately moved her to the rail, cutting off Champion. She was already on the lead, hugging the rail.

"Nice break for the filly," Ian said tersely.

Oh, no! Cindy slid to the edge of her seat. Sky Beauty had beaten Champion in the Florida Derby even when Champion had gone right to the lead. Now it looked like Sky Beauty had the jump on him—maybe for good. *All our plans for this race are already messed up!* she thought.

"And it's Sky Beauty on the lead; back two to Wonder's Champion," the announcer called. "Secret Sign is in third as they round the first turn. Back four to Greek Mystery, trailed by King Louie in fourth. . . ."

In the next instant Secret Sign charged up on Champion's outside.

"What is Shawn doing?" Cindy cried. "I thought Secret was a closer!"

"He's rating Secret in second," Mike said. He sounded nervous. "Shawn doesn't want to let Champion and Sky Beauty open up too much of a lead on him."

Cindy stared at the track, hardly daring to breathe. She had hoped against hope that Secret Sign and Champion wouldn't be running close together so soon—or at all. Now it looked like they would be running the whole race neck and neck. *This race is going to be tough*, she thought. *Sky Beauty is running incredibly well—she may not need to count on trouble from the colts to win it. Champion just has to run his best!* Cindy grabbed her binoculars as the field headed into the backstretch, trying to see if either colt was interfering with the other.

They weren't, but she saw a new problem. Champion and Secret Sign weren't fighting, but they were pressing the pace just behind Sky Beauty. "They won't leave her alone!" Cindy said in dismay. "Aren't they going too fast, Dad?"

Ian nodded without taking his eyes off the track. "Yes, but Ashleigh can't rate Champion any more. He's getting rank."

"Looks like Shawn is having the same problem with Secret Sign," Mike said.

"Sky Beauty is still maintaining her lead as they round the turn," the announcer called. "Wonder's Champion is in a hard-held second, with Secret Sign up close third. Blazing fractions here, folks. Forty-six seconds for the half."

Cindy bit her lip with worry. Champion was strong and fast, but she had no idea if he could keep up that pace to the wire. And he wasn't even on the lead. He had to come up with more speed!

Champion was running easily, almost gaily as the horses pounded into the stretch. He was extended but not straining, his dark mane and tail streaming out behind him. As he bounded along the rail the colt seemed to be ignoring Secret Sign.

Cindy felt a strong surge of hope. *I think he learned his lesson about leaving other horses alone,* she thought. *Now we just have to hope he's got the power and drive to win!*

"Sky Beauty may not be able to hold on in the last furlong," Ian shouted. "She's untried at a mile and a quarter."

"She looks pretty strong!" Cindy groaned. Champion was running out of time. It looked like Sky Beauty was going to take the Derby in a wire-to-wire finish!

Then Cindy saw that Sky Beauty was tiring. Her bay neck was dark with sweat. The game filly was giving the race her all, but she drifted out from the rail, blocking Champion and Secret Sign.

"Now, Ashleigh!" Cindy cried. "Go through!"

Suddenly Ashleigh made her move. But Shawn Biermont had seen the opening, too. Both colts lunged for the tiny hole on the rail.

"They've both got a closing kick," Cindy gasped. But Champion had more, although just barely! Champion squeezed through the hole ahead of him. At the last possible second Shawn was forced to check Secret Sign hard. Champion's strides propelled him airborne, until he seemed to hardly touch the ground. He was in the clear and pounding after Sky Beauty, in perfect striking position for the lead in the Kentucky Derby!

Sky Beauty was less than a length ahead. Champion drew up on the filly's flank. Champion's ears swept back.

Is he going after Sky Beauty or going for the lead? Cindy wondered desperately. "Run for it, Champion," she cried. "Run with everything you've got!"

The colt's nose stayed pointed straight ahead. He was going for the victory!

"Wonder's Champion loves to run at other horses, but he's not going to do it today," the announcer cried. "And they're into the final furlong!"

Champion was steadily gaining on Sky Beauty. The filly's ears flattened as Champion drew up at her shoulder. Sky Beauty was almost exhausted, but she was ready to die rather than give up the race!

"They're neck and neck with just seconds to the wire," the announcer shouted.

Cindy saw Nancy Keegan frantically kneading her filly's neck, asking for more. Sky Beauty's whole body was black with sweat, but she responded with a final courageous leap of speed.

"It's Sky Beauty by a nose," the announcer cried. "But Wonder's Champion is pressing hard . . . Griffen is asking her horse . . . and he sweeps to the lead! There's the wire! Wonder's Champion wins it!"

Cindy's knees were weak. In that instant before

the wire Champion had soared into his superdrive, that extra speed that no horse could beat. "He had more," she said. Happy tears were running down her face. "There's never been a horse like him!"

"He's the best, sweetie." Beth hugged her. "You've worked so hard for this."

Cindy smiled, brushing away her tears. "Let's go see him!"

The winner's circle was a blur for Cindy. She held the prancing, happy colt with her dad and Ashleigh and smiled for the TV cameras when the reporters yelled to her. Champion was blanketed in beautiful red roses, but instead of admiring them he tried to eat them. Cindy could barely keep his head straight for the cameras.

Suddenly Cindy focused on a reporter standing to the edge of the crowd. *That's the guy who laughed last summer when I said that Champion would win the Kentucky Derby!* she remembered.

Champion had managed to grab a rose from his blanket.

"Champion, no," Ashleigh said, smiling as she reached for the rose. The colt backed away and playfully tossed it, as if they were in the paddock and millions of people weren't watching.

Cindy caught the rose and touched it to her cheek. *Who's laughing now?* she thought happily.

"Champion's such a star," Mandy said. She had come over to visit Cindy at Whitebrook three days after the

Kentucky Derby. Mandy sighed. "I wish I had a star horse."

"You're jumping one of Tor's horses, right?" Cindy asked. She slid down farther on the stoop of her family's cottage and tilted back her head to let the sun fall on her face. *What a great day*, she thought. *But every day's been great since Champion won the Derby!*

The paddocks everywhere she looked were filled with beautiful Thoroughbreds, eagerly grazing the thick bluegrass and clover. Cindy could make out Glory's elegant gray silhouette at the back of one of the stallion paddocks, and Glory's Joy, a tiny, dark version of her sire, was romping with the nine other foals in the front paddock. Kevin and Christina played in a sandbox in the sideyard, their cries clear in the warm afternoon air. *It really feels good to be home*, Cindy thought.

"Yeah, Tennessee Cider is one of Tor's best horses." Mandy poked at the ground with a stick. "Tor's got me jumping up to four feet with him. Cider's nice, but it's not like having my own horse."

"I know what you mean." Sometimes Cindy felt that way about Champion. She exercised him and took care of him, but Ashleigh got to ride him in his races. *But now that Champion's a Derby winner, he belongs to the whole world!* Cindy thought. She smiled.

"I'm still looking for my dream horse," Mandy said. "I know that horse is out there somewhere."

"So's mine." Cindy got up and stretched. She couldn't stand doing nothing for long. "Champion's at the track, but he'll be home this winter. I can look forward to that."

"I'll probably be stuck in a snowdrift this winter, trying to find my horse," Mandy muttered.

"Let's go see the foals," Cindy suggested. "It's rained so much lately, I haven't been able to play with them for days." *If Mandy doesn't quit talking about her dream horse, I'm going to go nuts!* she thought. *She'll never find a horse that's good enough. Mandy's standards are so high, I think she's looking for a unicorn.*

Mandy brightened immediately. "I'd love to play with the babies!" She winced as she stood up.

"What's the matter?" Cindy asked.

"Oh, nothing." Mandy shrugged. "My legs hurt after I sit still for too long."

"They always do?" Cindy asked with concern.

"Yeah, I guess." Mandy was already walking toward the foals' paddock, limping slightly.

Wow, that's tough! Cindy thought. *But Mandy seems to handle it.*

In the front paddock all the foals froze as the girls approached. Some stood by their mothers. A few were by themselves, scattered across the paddock, their long legs splayed as they looked up from their grazing. A group of foals had stopped frolicking across the thick emerald grass to stare at Cindy and Mandy. Cindy smiled at the trusting, inquisitive expressions in the foals' dark eyes.

Glory's Joy was one of the foals who had been romping. She cocked her head and gazed at the girls, as if she couldn't decide who would make livelier playmates, the other foals or the humans.

"Come here, little girl," Cindy coaxed, holding out her hand.

Joy's ears pricked, then she stepped confidently forward. Cindy loved the feel of the baby's soft, whiskery muzzle as Joy gently lipped her hand.

"This is too fun," Mandy said with a grin. The other foals had surrounded her and were nudging her and bumping each other as they begged for attention. Mandy was patting two at a time, working her way around the circle.

"I guess they know Joy's my favorite, so they went over to you." Cindy felt a little guilty. But she couldn't seem to stop running her hand over Joy's thick, silken coat or looking at the perfectly conformed almost black baby.

The small foal let out a half sigh, half whicker. Cindy sighed, too. *Joy seems to be such a sweet gray horse, like Storm was*, she thought. *I hope you do all right on the track.* Champion, with his bold personality and love of the limelight, seemed perfectly suited to be a racehorse.

"I wish I were back with Champion," Cindy said to Mandy. The younger girl was so short, Cindy could hardly see her at the center of the crowd of foals. Already the young horses were taller even than Cindy. "The Derby pressure is off now—but Champion's still got two Triple Crown races to go," she added.

"You'll be back with him in a week or so," Mandy

said. "He should be okay till then." She laughed as Zero's Flight, one of the bolder colts, almost knocked her over into the circle of foals. "Hanging out here is pretty good."

"We've got a surprise for you, Cindy," Max said mysteriously on a Saturday night four days later. Cindy, Max, Heather, and Doug had just gotten out of Samantha's car and were walking to the school gym for the big end-of-school dance they had helped plan.

"What's the surprise—more rain?" Cindy asked as she ran through the drops, trying to stay under Max's umbrella. She glanced up at the sky. Heavy black clouds scudded across it, and rain slanted sideways in the glow from the streetlights. The entire East Coast had been nearly flooded for weeks from storms.

Cindy just hoped the rain cleared off soon so that the track would dry out for the Preakness next Saturday. Otherwise Champion would have to run in the mud, and she had no idea how he would handle it.

"What we've got in mind is even better than more rain," Heather teased. "Wait till you see."

Cindy stopped to catch her breath in front of the gym, out of the pounding rain. She tried to smooth her hair.

"Great," she said. "I'm glad we spent two hours fixing our hair, Heather. And my dress has polka dots." Cindy had taken a lot of time picking out her dress. She hadn't had much choice—Heather had carefully searched every store in the mall, looking for the perfect outfit for herself.

Cindy had to admit the result of all that work was good. She wore a bright navy print sundress with a small matching jacket and navy espadrilles. Max had already complimented her on her looks twice.

"Don't worry; the paint's waterproof," Heather said, smiling.

Cindy wondered if she'd heard right. "Excuse me? Heather, has the rain messed up your hair and your mind?"

Heather laughed. "Look above you."

Cindy looked up—and her mouth dropped open in astonishment. A huge banner hanging over the doorway to the gym said, GOOD LUCK, CHAMPION— OUR NEXT TRIPLE CROWN WINNER! Underneath the lettering was a detailed, lifelike drawing of a dark chestnut horse, blazing across the finish at a racetrack. White letters across the track said Belmont.

"Wow!" Cindy exclaimed. "Somehow I just know you had something to do with this, Heather. Not because I recognize your handwriting or artwork or anything."

"We all did." Max grinned.

"Come on inside," Doug said. "The show's just beginning."

Cindy stepped into the gym, and her hands flew to her cheeks. The large room had been lavishly decorated with blue, white, and brown streamers and helium balloons. Banners hung everywhere. Her eyes

161

wide with astonishment, Cindy read a few: Cindy's Champion; Ashleigh's Wonder—Dam of Champions; Wonder's Champion—Horse of the Year.

In the center of the refreshment table was a thickly frosted, three-foot-long chocolate cake. "Isn't that the biggest cake you ever saw?" Doug asked. "It's for the whole ninth-grade class."

"Because we're all cheering you and Champion on," Heather said.

"This is . . . you guys . . ." Cindy sputtered. She couldn't believe her friends had gone to so much trouble and were being so supportive.

"Of course you know why the room's decorated in brown, blue, and white," Heather said, steering a dazed Cindy to the refreshment table.

"No," Cindy said, trying to catch her breath. Max handed her a cup of punch.

"Because blue and white are Whitebrook's racing colors, and Champion is dark brown, silly," Heather replied, laughing. "I thought everybody knew that."

Laura, Sharon, Melissa, and several of Cindy's other friends crowded around her. "Good luck at the Preakness, Cindy," Melissa said. "How's Champion doing?"

"He's raring to go." Cindy smiled. Champion had shipped to the Pimlico track in Maryland, the site of the Preakness, a few days earlier. With just two weeks between the Kentucky Derby and the Preakness, Ashleigh, Mike, and Ian had been eager to get Champion up to the Maryland track and begin his workouts there.

Ashleigh had called the night before to reassure Cindy that the colt was just fine. Ashleigh's only worry was the weather. With the almost constant rain, they'd had to restrict Champion's workouts. But Cindy knew that the other horses entered in the Preakness were suffering under the same conditions.

"We're rooting for you, Cindy," Melissa said seriously. "This is exciting for all of us. Champion's a Kentucky bred."

"Are you going to the Preakness?" Cindy asked. "If you are, maybe I'll see you there." Melissa and her family often went to the bigger races.

Melissa nodded. "We'll leave Friday. We don't have a horse running, though."

"Hey, take *me* to the Preakness," Laura joked. "Or Chelsea—she's dying to see a horse, any horse."

"She can come over to Whitebrook again soon," Cindy said. "Once school is out, I should have more time." Cindy had been so busy with Champion and her regular chores, she hadn't been able to spend as much time with Chelsea as she would have liked. Chelsea had come over twice since her raffle ride.

"Hey, this is a dance, remember?" Max said. "Why are we all standing around?"

"Are you asking me to dance?" Cindy smiled.

Max pretended to consider. "I guess I was."

He held out his hand, and they walked out onto the dance floor. A local band was playing some of Cindy's favorite songs. In moments Cindy was laughing as Max swung her around in an energetic version of the two-step. Max was a very good dancer, and Cindy noticed that a lot of the girls were watching him. A few asked to cut in, and Cindy reluctantly let them.

After a couple of fast songs the band began a slow number. The lights dimmed. Max left Laura and walked over to Cindy, who was waiting at the edge of the dance floor.

"Should we dance this one?" he asked. Flushed with excitement, Cindy nodded. She had enjoyed slow dancing with Max at the last dance. *I guess I feel a lot more comfortable with Max these days*, she said to herself.

Cindy hesitated, then stepped closer to Max. He put his arms around her, and they moved slowly in time to the music. Cindy could feel a smile stealing across her lips, and she sighed softly with contentment. *We dance so well together*, she thought.

"Do you like your party?" Max asked.

"I love it," Cindy said sincerely. "You guys went to so much trouble."

"Too bad the other guest of honor can't be here . . . Champion, I mean," Max commented.

"I'll tell him all about it when I see him next week," Cindy promised, floating in time to the music.

This feels like a dream, she thought, smiling up into Max's green eyes. *But it isn't—it's just the most perfect evening ever.*

13

A WEEK LATER, ON THE SATURDAY OF THE PREAKNESS, CINDY walked beside Champion and Len in driving rain to the saddling paddock. She hadn't gotten her wish that the rain would stop—far from it. Storms had battered the East Coast all week, and the Pimlico track was listed as muddy. Cindy knew there was no way the track condition would change before race time.

"Len, I'm just so afraid Champion's going to have a lot of trouble out there," Cindy said quietly.

"He doesn't know it." Len placed his weathered hand on Champion's neck as they walked along.

Cindy's spirits brightened as she looked at the colt. Champion was prancing along, slopping through puddles as if they weren't there. He was covered against the rain with a blue-and-white sheet, and the wet cloth just accentuated his bunchy muscles. Five days ago Champion had put in a bullet work at three-quarters of a mile. "You're not expecting any trouble today, are you?" she asked affectionately.

Champion splattered cheerfully through another puddle, sending a tidal wave of cold, wet water into Cindy's boot. She grimaced. *This weather is the pits,* she thought. *The last time Champion ran on a muddy track, he lost—in the Kentucky Cup Juvenile Stakes last fall.* She knew, too, that Pride had lost the Preakness on a muddy track, ending Whitebrook's Triple Crown dreams that year.

In the saddling paddock Len held the colt while Ian swiftly placed the colt's saddlepad, cloth, and racing saddle on his back. "Let's go," Ian said.

Cindy patted Champion's wet neck. "You're ready, aren't you, boy?" she asked. "It's just the people who aren't sure."

Ashleigh was waiting patiently for the colt in the walking ring. The rain had already soaked her, but she wasn't making any effort to shield herself. Cindy figured Ashleigh thought there was no point, since she'd be out on the track in the mud and rain in a few minutes anyway.

"Hey, Champion," Ashleigh greeted the colt. "Another big race, boy. But we're used to them."

"I just don't know how he'll do on this off footing." Mike's forehead was creased with worry.

Cindy glanced at Ashleigh. Cindy hadn't wanted to bring up the obvious dangers of the track today, but she wondered what Ashleigh thought.

Ashleigh quickly mounted up and looked down at the concerned faces surrounding her. She smiled. "Don't worry, everybody. Champion's going to give it his all—I'm sure of that. He's our Champion, right?"

Cindy nodded, swallowing a lump in her throat. *So are you, Ashleigh,* she thought as she watched the jockey confidently walk Champion toward the track. The fog swiftly swallowed them up.

In the stands Cindy huddled under a large umbrella with Samantha. The rain had stopped, but the heavy fog completely clouded the track. Cindy could see Champion moving in and out of the streamers of fog like a dream horse, not quite real.

"Champion's workouts have been good in the mud," Samantha remarked.

"I know. And he's drawn a good position," Cindy said hopefully. "Three isn't bad in a field of eleven."

"It seems good to me." Beth smiled encouragingly at Cindy.

"We'll just have to see how Champion does today," Ian said.

Cindy blew out a nervous breath. The field was distinguished, but Champion had beaten several of the horses before. Secret Sign was running that day, too. Cindy wasn't worried that the colts would fight—Champion seemed to have gotten over his dislike of the other colt. But Secret Sign was always a strong contender, and Cindy had a new concern about him today. The gray colt was a mudder—he had won three races on muddy tracks.

Champion just has to run well in the mud today, Cindy thought. *I wish the weather could have been good for all the Triple Crown races! But I guess that was too much to hope for.*

The horses were led to the gate. Cindy winced as Candy Sweetheart, a black Florida bred, slipped in the mud. Champion walked right into the gate and stood calmly.

"With this much fog, we won't be able to see most of the race," Mike commented. "Just part of the turns and the stretch."

"We'll listen to the announcer." Beth squeezed Cindy's hand.

Cindy nodded, trying to relax. She put down the umbrella so that she could see better. The air was so moist and sticky, the umbrella wasn't helping much anyway. *Champion can handle an off track*, she assured herself. *He's strong, and he knows what he's doing.*

The bell clanged, sounding muffled in the thick air. "And they're off on a muddy racetrack," the announcer called. "Secret Sign is away quickly, followed by Roaring Twenties. Wonder's Champion is right there in third. Back three to Say No More as they head into the first turn."

"Champion's not on the lead!" Cindy ran her hands nervously through her damp hair. "He'll be taking so much mud in his face. He won't like being behind horses either!"

"He's not dropping back, though," Ian said. Like Cindy, her dad was half out of his seat, straining to see through the fog.

"Champion isn't letting the mud stop him," Samantha said.

Cindy wondered desperately if that was true. For whatever reason Champion hadn't been first out of the gate. He was clearly struggling with the surface, but so were the other horses. Cindy bit back a cry as Say No More, a big California colt, skidded across the track to the inside, nearly colliding with Champion.

"Wonder's Champion is sent through an opening on the rail as they head into the turn," the announcer said.

"Ashleigh didn't send him." Mike was shaking his head. "Champion's fighting Ashleigh and is going to the rail on his own!"

"What's wrong with that?" Cindy asked. "Wasn't he just getting out of Say No More's Way?" She could barely see the horses as they rounded the turn. Then they faded into the mist, and Champion was gone.

"The rail has been dead all day," Mike answered.

"Oh, no!" Cindy stared at Mike. She couldn't see anything on the track, anyway. The Preakness was a mile and three-sixteenths. Cindy didn't know if Champion could fight Ashleigh and the surface and still have enough left to win the race. The mud was so tiring.

Cindy stood on tiptoe, trying to penetrate the blanket of fog. It was frustrating not to be able to see the colt.

"There's half a mile to run," the announcer said. "Secret Sign is still on the lead by half a length. But

169

Wonder's Champion is moving right with him. Back five to Say No More; racing in fourth is Candy Sweetheart. . . ."

What's Champion doing? Cindy wondered frantically. *Is he still fighting Ashleigh? He's keeping up, but he's still in second! Does he have more left?*

At that instant Champion burst out of the silvery fog. A dark torpedo of power and sheer will to win, he roared by Secret Sign on the inside. Cindy let out a whoop of joy.

"And Wonder's Champion takes the lead at the top of the stretch!" the announcer called.

"Go!" Cindy screamed. "Keep it up, boy!"

Champion was slowly drawing off from the other colt. He was a neck ahead, then, with agonizing slowness, half a length. Cindy could almost feel Champion's effort as he struggled for traction on the slippery surface.

"It's so hard for him to drive through the mud!" she cried.

"But he's doing it!" Samantha sounded breathless.

"Wonder's Champion is trying to hold on," the announcer said. "But Secret Sign is closing. They're neck and neck—Secret Sign is ahead by a nose!"

Champion, go into your superdrive! Cindy cried silently. *But maybe you already are just to get through the mud.* "Please, Champion," she called. "Give just a little more!"

As if he had heard, Champion made one last valiant effort, his hooves digging deep into the soggy, slippery ground. He inched up on Secret Sign. Champion's nose was in front!

"Yes!" Cindy screeched. "You've got it. Just another second, boy!" The wire approached as Champion battled to hang on. Secret Sign was slowly moving up again. The colts strained side by side, each fiercely determined to win. But the wire flashed overhead. Champion was under it first!

"Wonder's Champion proves just good enough!" the announcer cried. "He wins the second leg of the Triple Crown."

Cindy sank down in her wet chair, overwhelmed. She knew Champion had never run so hard in his life. "He won!" she whispered. She had imagined this moment so many times for the past two weeks, it was hard for her to believe it was real.

Samantha touched Cindy's arm. "Let's get down to the winner's circle," she said. "It's not every day that a horse wins two races of the Triple Crown, even a Whitebrook horse!"

"I know." Cindy jumped up, a quick, delicious sense of bliss stealing through her. Champion was so important now—so famous! With wins like these, his future as a stud at Whitebrook was assured.

On the track Ashleigh was surrounded by the press and well-wishers, all clamoring for a statement. Ashleigh stopped for a moment to speak to them, then made her way through the crowd toward the winner's circle.

"Champion, you were wonderful!" Cindy cried, going immediately to the colt's head.

Champion was light brown with mud, from his eyelids to the end of his tail. He blinked and shook himself, showering the onlookers with sticky mud. Patches of his dark brown coat showed through. "Now I can see a little of you," Cindy said, laughing. Champion had missed her with the worst of the mud, but she wouldn't have minded if he hadn't. *I'd keep it as a souvenir!* she thought.

Cindy gave Champion a quick, expert once-over. The colt's sides were heaving and his nostrils showed red. But that wasn't surprising, given the strain that race had been. "I'll make it up to you, sweetie," she said, taking the colt's muddy head in her arms. "Don't worry."

Champion leaned on her gratefully. *For once he really seems tired,* she realized.

Ashleigh had noticed, too. "Let's get Champion cleaned up a little and let the press take a few photographs," she said. "Then we'll head to the backside and take care of him."

Cindy looked up quickly and found herself staring directly into a TV camera. For a moment she had forgotten that she and Champion were standing in the winner's circle at a famous track, surrounded by a mob. "I can't believe you pulled that race out!" she whispered to Ashleigh as Len put a clean saddlecloth on the colt's back.

"Me neither," Ashleigh said ruefully. "At the half-mile pole he dragged me to the rail, and that made a lot of extra work for us. But maybe he knew what he was doing!"

"It looks that way." Cindy was all smiles. Champion had done a fine job, and she couldn't be prouder.

The cameras flashed as Champion stood in the winner's circle, blanketed with the traditional black-eyed Susans for winning the Preakness. Cindy gently touched one of the black-and-yellow flowers. *I'll take one for my Triple Crown scrapbook,* she thought. Cindy already had a red rose from the Kentucky Derby. All she needed now was a Belmont white carnation.

"Okay, that's enough," Ashleigh said good-naturedly to the press, handing Champion's lead line to Cindy. "We need to cool out our colt."

Cindy stayed close to Champion as Ian led the colt toward the backside. Track police cleared a path for them. *Champion's such a star,* Cindy thought, bursting with pride.

"After a race like today's, I'm confident about our chances in the Belmont," Cindy heard Ashleigh say to a reporter.

Cindy turned to Champion. For just a second she was a little shocked by how dirty and tired he looked. But Champion nudged her firmly, the way he always did, as if to tell her that under all that mud he was still himself.

"What do you say to that, boy?" she asked. "We'll get you ready for the Belmont over the next couple of weeks. But first let's give you a nice warm bath to get that mud off, then a good dinner, with a carrot appetizer."

The beautiful colt bobbed his head, as if to say he was ready for a little R and R after his effort.

Cindy looked at Champion carefully as the colt followed her dad. She was still a little worried about him, but probably a good rest was all he needed.

Suddenly her heart almost stopped. *I have to be imagining this*, she thought. But after Champion took a few more steps, she knew she wasn't. Champion was favoring one of his legs. "Dad, Champion's limping!" she cried.

Ian immediately stopped the colt. "Which leg is it?" he asked, stepping back from Champion.

"I—I think it's his right fore." Cindy blinked back panicky tears. *Stay calm and help*, she ordered herself. Usually Cindy could easily tell which foot a horse was favoring, but now she could hardly think straight. Champion was injured. She knew that the colt's chances of winning the Belmont—and the Triple Crown—had probably just ended.

"He may only be stiff," Ian said. "Hold him, Cindy, while I look at his legs."

Numb with fear, Cindy clutched Champion's lead rope and twisted it in her hands. Not seeming in the least perturbed, Champion nibbled at her hands, looking for carrots. "Do you see anything?" Cindy asked her dad.

Ian had worked his way around Champion's four legs to his right fore. "No . . . not yet. Ah, here it is."

"What's wrong?" Cindy asked, trying to steady her voice.

"He's got a cut in the bulb of his hoof." Ian lifted his head. "Good, here comes Len. We've got to get this cleaned up right away. Let's get Champion back to the barn, out of the rain."

"Is it bad?" Cindy's teeth were chattering. She was wet clear through, but that wasn't why she was shaking.

"No, not at all," Ian said soothingly.

"But I guess he won't be starting in the Belmont." Cindy wiped her eyes with the back of her hand. The rain was really coming down again. She couldn't tell if her eyes were wet from the rain or tears.

"We'll see," Ian replied. "It's too soon to tell."

"Come on, big guy," Len said. "Come on with me, and we'll get you fixed up."

In the stall the colt twisted his head, trying to see Len, who was washing off the injured foot. Cindy rubbed his neck vigorously to distract him. "Just stay still, boy," she said. "This will be over in a minute. You'll hurt yourself more if you put down your hoof."

Champion eyed her. Then he pushed his muddy head against the nice shirt Cindy had worn for the winner's circle pictures. He seemed to be saying, *This is a tradeoff.*

"Okay, Champion—my shirt's probably wrecked anyway at this point," Cindy said with a sigh.

Ian bandaged the cut while Len covered the colt with a warm blanket. Cindy smoothed Champion's muddy mane, trying not to jump to conclusions.

"What happened?" Ashleigh stood beside Cindy,

still wearing her wet jockey silks. A moment later Mike joined her.

"Champion's got a superficial cut," Ian said, gently lowering the colt's bandaged hoof to the ground.

Mike and Ashleigh said nothing, but Cindy saw their grim expressions.

"Can I cool him out now?" Cindy asked. She wanted to do something for Champion.

"I think he's probably cooled out enough from the walk back to the barn," Ian said. "I'll call the horseshoer. He can put on a shoe that will take the weight off Champion's injury."

"Then I'll just give him a bath." Cindy filled a bucket with warm water and sponged Champion off, then dried him thoroughly. After she had combed out his mane and tail, the colt looked like himself again. Cindy noticed that he wasn't holding the weight off his injured right front hoof. *That's good—at least he isn't in pain*, she thought. But she wondered how that hoof would feel when he ran.

"This really throws a kink in things," Ashleigh said to Mike and Ian. "Should we still take Champion to Belmont on Thursday, the way we planned?"

"I think so," Mike said.

Cindy looked out of the stall. "Is it safe to van him?" she asked.

"Of course," Ashleigh said. "Champion's injury isn't that bad, Cindy." She frowned. "The problem is, any injury is bad right now. We've got only three weeks until the Belmont."

Cindy nodded. Champion would have to recover from his injury and at the same time get in shape for the longest race of his life.

The colt poked his head out of the stall, looking over the top of her head. Cindy reached up to rub his blaze.

"This is going to be a real fight, boy," she said. "But we're in it together."

14

CINDY HAD PLANNED TO RETURN TO WHITEBROOK FOR A few days in between the Belmont and the Preakness. She had wanted to work with Honor Bright and ride Glory, and enjoy a short time away from the bustling, fast-paced life at the track. But now that Champion was injured, Cindy decided to go immediately to Belmont with the colt. Ashleigh, Mike, and Ian would travel with him, too.

Four days after the Preakness the Whitebrook group left Pimlico. After a long, worrisome van ride, Cindy settled Champion in his stall at Belmont. The colt had traveled like a pro, and he seemed comfortable in his new stall.

Every day Cindy helped with Champion's treatment. Before the colt left Pimlico, a horseshoer had fitted him with a special bar shoe to take the weight off his injury. The cut had to be soaked daily to prevent infection.

"Champion really doesn't like that water, does he?" Len said one morning two weeks after the Preakness. Cindy was soaking the colt's hoof in a bucket.

"No, he hates doing this." The colt had just yanked his leg out of the bucket for the tenth time. Cindy grabbed it before his hoof could touch the ground and gently lowered it back into the warm water. "But I think Champion hates standing still for so long more than the water. He's never been injured before. . . ." Cindy bit her lip.

"Let me see his hoof." Len picked up Champion's right foot and carefully examined the heel. "It's healing up well," he said. "No sign of infection."

"It looked good to me, too." Cindy knew that infection was what they all feared. As long as the colt's hoof stayed healthy, he would remain entered in the Belmont. But at the first sign of infection he would have to be scratched.

Cindy blew out a tired breath and removed Champion's foot from the bucket. "Okay, you're done, boy. How about some grass?" Champion shook himself thoroughly, then glanced at her brightly. Cindy had to laugh at the colt's eager expression. *He sure is a spunky colt,* she thought.

She walked Champion out to the stable yard to graze. The weather had brightened but remained cool, and it was more like fall than June in New York.

This is perfect racing weather, she thought, looking at Champion with longing. *I just hope it stays that way—and you get to run!*

Ashleigh had kept the colt in light training since his injury. Cindy knew that Ashleigh had no choice—Champion couldn't run in the Belmont cold, after three weeks off. The morning before Ashleigh had galloped him. Champion had seemed okay, but Cindy knew the real test would be when he was asked to run. Tomorrow Ashleigh would work the colt for the first time since the Preakness and his injury.

"Hey, Cindy—look what I've got for you," Samantha called.

Startled out of her thoughts, Cindy looked up. Samantha was walking toward her, holding a small bouquet of carnations.

"Who are they from?" Cindy asked in surprise.

"I don't know." Samantha handed her the flowers. "Read the card."

Cindy took the lovely flowers and opened the card—they were from Max! *White carnations will be around Champion's neck in a week when he wins the Belmont,* Max had written. *See you soon!* Cindy was touched by his thoughtfulness.

"Who are they from?" Samantha asked.

"Max. He said he'd see me soon—but I don't know what he meant. He's in Kentucky." Cindy deeply inhaled the warm, summery scent of the flowers.

"Well, Dr. Smith is coming to Belmont," Samantha said. "She's going to take care of Champion."

"So Max must be coming, too!" Cindy was thrilled. *It'll be great to have Max here when I'm so worried about Champion,* she thought.

"Really soon," Samantha said with a grin. "He's right over there. He was watching me deliver the flowers."

"Surprise!" Max stepped out from behind a tree and walked across the stable yard. "Hey, Champion— how's the big bad horse?" Champion jerked up his head from the grass, seeming to know exactly who Max was talking about. The colt stepped sociably close to Max and sniffed his hands. Max pulled a carrot out of his jeans, then patted Champion's forehead as the colt crunched.

"Max, I can't believe you're here!" Cindy smiled. "Champion's fine—we're pretty sure he isn't going to get an infection." Cindy had filled in all her friends back home about Champion's condition. "The only thing we don't know is whether he can run or not." She looked quickly at Max. "Is your mom here just to treat Champion?"

Max shook his head. "That's a big reason, but she's got other clients here, too."

Cindy was relieved. As much as she liked Dr. Smith, it wasn't usually a good sign when the vet showed up.

Champion snatched at the bouquet with his teeth. "No, Champion, these aren't for you!" Cindy held the flowers out of his reach. "Or maybe they are, but you're not supposed to eat them," she amended. "Thanks for the flowers, Max."

"No problem," Max assured her. Champion eyed Cindy. He seemed to be thinking about making another try for the flowers. Then he huffed out a sigh, as if he knew it was no use, and dropped his head back to the grass.

"Do you want me to take Champion while you and Max get caught up?" Samantha asked.

"I guess." Cindy was reluctant to leave the colt.

"Go on," Samantha urged. "Take a break. You've practically been living with Champion."

"Are you sleeping in the stall again?" Max asked.

Cindy shook her head. "No, not yet. My parents won't let me stay there until a few days before the race." Cindy had argued that one for a long time, but her parents had held firm.

Samantha reached for Champion's lead line. "See you later," she said.

"Let's look around the shed rows, the way we always do," Max said.

"Okay." Cindy glanced distractedly at Champion, but she nodded. Every time Cindy and Max were at racetracks together, they had made it a tradition to walk around the backside, looking at the horses.

Max was smiling at her. She smiled back. *I'll bet this is the first time I've smiled in a week!* she thought. *I shouldn't worry so much—it's not going to help.*

"Which barn should we start with?" Max asked.

Cindy thought a moment. In the ten days she had been at Belmont, she'd been too busy with Champion to look around much. Taking care of Limitless Time,

Freedom's Ring, and the three other Whitebrook horses already at the track for the summer races had also kept her busy. "Let's go see Silk Stockings," she said. "He just shipped in from Kentucky. Everyone's saying he's going to be a real contender in the race."

As Cindy walked away Champion lifted his head and stared at her, as if to say, *Just where are you going?*

"I'll be back soon, Champion," Cindy promised. "Behave yourself while I'm gone, if that's possible." She led the way to Silk Stockings' shed row, ignoring Champion's piercing, outraged whinny at her neglect.

"Why is Silk Stockings getting so much attention?" Max asked.

"He won the Blue Grass and a couple of other important Kentucky Derby prep races," Cindy said. "But he didn't run in the Derby because he strained a tendon right before it. Like Champion, he's coming off an injury."

Cindy caught a glimpse of Silk Stockings, who was being led back to the shed row by a groom. With his four white stockings and imperious walk, the big chestnut was unmistakable. But before Cindy could follow him, she was stopped by a young, dark-haired reporter. "How's Champion doing?" the woman asked, flipping open her notebook.

"Just fine," Cindy replied politely.

"What do you think his chances are in the race?" the reporter asked.

"I'm sorry, but I don't have any comment at this

time." Cindy walked quickly toward the shed row. She saw other reporters, notebooks and cameras in hand, heading her way and ducked inside.

"Why didn't you want to talk to that reporter?" Max asked, running to catch up.

"I'm not supposed to without my dad or somebody else around." Cindy shrugged. "I have to be careful what I tell them. A lot of times what Ashleigh or my dad says appears on the front page of the next day's newspaper. I don't want to start any rumors about Champion's health."

Max nodded. "At least they didn't follow you in here."

"Yeah, good. There's Silk Stockings." Cindy pointed to the end of the shed row. The colt had just had a bath, and his groom was drying him off.

Cindy narrowed her eyes thoughtfully. Even from a distance Silk Stockings' toned muscles, defined by his wet coat, told her the colt was in top shape. *He must be completely over his injury*, she thought. *I just hope Champion is.* "Nice," she said to Max. "I guess I've seen what I needed to."

Max jammed his hands into his pockets. "He looks tough," he commented. "Who's next?"

"I just want to see City Lady; then I'd better get back to Champion," she said. "City Lady is the only filly running in the Belmont. She's in the next barn over."

City Lady was in her stall, tossing her head impatiently. The light chestnut laid back her ears a fraction as Max and Cindy approached.

"She's like Champion—she doesn't let just anybody get close," Max commented.

"If Champion weren't running, I'd root for City Lady." Cindy smiled at the fire in City's Lady's eyes. "A filly hasn't won the Belmont for almost a century."

"Well, City Lady's trainer must think she can win it, or he wouldn't have entered her in the race," Max remarked.

"That's true. But none of these horses can hold a candle to Champion when he's at his best," Cindy said confidently. "I just have to make sure he's at the top of his game on race day."

The next morning Ian had scheduled Champion to work out for the first time since the colt's injury. Cindy stood tensely at the rail with Max, hardly daring to breathe as Ashleigh trotted Champion around the track. Limitless Time, ridden by Samantha, was already warming up on the track. The two colts would work together.

The morning was cool but sticky—summer had crept back to New York after the heavy spring rains. The pale blue sky seemed faded by the humidity. *Champion won't mind hot weather*, Cindy said to herself. *He's a Kentucky horse. At least that's one thing I don't have to worry about.*

Ashleigh pulled Champion up at the gap. "Okay," she said. "I'm going to work him three-eighths of a mile."

"Are you sure it's all right?" Cindy bit her cuticle from worry as she looked up at Champion. The colt was cheerfully tossing his head, as if he couldn't wait to get going. *You don't know what can go wrong, boy,* Cindy thought.

"I think so," Ashleigh said gently. "But I have to work him, Cindy. We don't want to wait any longer— it's only a week till the race. His hoof's not going to get much better in a day or two."

Cindy nodded. She couldn't argue with that. But as Ashleigh moved Champion down the rail to talk to Ian and Mike, Cindy suddenly wished that she could just take Champion home. *I was more excited about Champion's winning the Triple Crown than anything in my life, but working him seems like such a risk,* she thought.

Max squeezed her hand. "It's okay," he said, as if he could read her thoughts. "Ashleigh knows what she's doing."

"Sure." Cindy closed her eyes for a second, willing herself to be brave. Ashleigh and Samantha had trotted Champion and Limitless to the far side of the track. At Ashleigh's signal the two horses burst into a gallop, skimming the rail. Champion was slightly in front of the black colt as they soared around the far turn.

"So far, so good," Max said. "Champion's got a great way of going."

"Yeah, but they haven't really started to run yet." Cindy let go of Max's hand. Her own hand was starting to sweat.

At the three-eighths pole both Ashleigh and Samantha moved their hands up on the colts' necks and crouched forward, asking for speed.

Here we go! Cindy thought, leaning forward herself. As many times as she had seen horses work, Cindy had always thrilled to that magic instant when a racing Thoroughbred roared into high gear, running his heart out the way he had been bred to do.

Champion was beautiful as he ran against Limitless Time. His chocolate mane and tail streamed behind him, strikingly dark against the soft colors of the summer landscape. Cindy couldn't see anything wrong with Champion's strides. They were full, even, and graceful, as always.

But as the horses galloped into the stretch Cindy's breath caught in her throat. Limitless Time was overtaking Champion!

"I don't believe it!" she gasped. "Limitless has never beat Champion for a second before."

"Maybe Champion will catch him at the finish." Max sounded anxious, too.

But Champion fell back another length, then two lengths. The colts flashed by the gap. Champion had been beaten by three lengths!

Cindy was so shocked, she felt as if someone had hit her on the head. "Champion must still be hurt!" she said. Cindy waited in agony as Ashleigh galloped Champion out a furlong, then trotted him back to the gap. *What if he hurt himself more?* she thought.

Ashleigh jumped out of the saddle and shook her

head. "He never really kicked in," she said. "Let's take a look at that hoof." Ashleigh, Mike, and Ian crowded around Champion, and Ian picked up the colt's right front hoof.

Despite her worry Cindy noticed that Champion was eating up all the attention. He bent his head to touch each of the humans kneeling around him, lipping at shirts, pants pockets, and hair. "You silly guy," Cindy said, her voice breaking. Champion snorted with pleasure.

"I don't see anything wrong." Ian straightened up and put Champion's hoof back on the ground. "The bar shoe seems to be in place, too."

"Maybe Champion just needs to get used to the shoe," Ashleigh said. "I'll gallop him later in the week. Why don't you take him back to the barn for now, Cindy?"

"Sure thing." Cindy stretched her hand for the colt's reins. She could tell Ashleigh was trying to sound upbeat. Cindy reminded herself not to be a bad sport and seem down in the dumps.

Champion stepped willingly toward her. *At least he doesn't seem to mind moving,* she noted with relief. *He can't be in too much pain.*

"The press is going wild, speculating about whether we'll run Champion or not," Mike remarked.

"We'll make the decision closer to the race." Ashleigh shrugged. "Of course we won't run him if we think he can't win or if his hoof still seems to be a problem."

188

Cindy nodded grimly. Handing Champion's reins to her dad for a moment, she stepped over to pat Limitless Time, who Samantha had just ridden off the track. "He ran well," Cindy said, trying to smile. She couldn't fault Limitless for Champion's loss.

Samantha nodded. "He did. That was a very good time. Champion didn't run badly, Cindy. . . ."

Cindy nodded. *But he still lost!* she thought.

"What do you think happened?" Max asked as he and Cindy led Champion toward the backside.

"I think Champion's superdrive is missing." Cindy's stomach churned. "I don't know if his foot is still hurting. He may be afraid to run really fast if he's in even a little pain. Or Ashleigh may be right that the bar shoe is messing him up. But what worries me most . . ." Cindy tried to steady her voice. "Champion's superdrive was so special. It may just be gone now that he's gotten hurt. He may have lost that extra edge."

"Champion could get better before the race," Max said. "You've still got a week."

"Yeah." Cindy tried not to sound discouraged. "We probably won't know anything more until then."

"I've got to meet my mom now, but I'll come back later," Max said sympathetically.

"Okay. I'd better take care of Champion." Cindy turned determinedly to the colt. Champion was standing still, gently switching his tail to brush off flies. *I almost wish he'd act up, the way he usually does,* Cindy said to herself. Champion hardly ever waited patiently for anyone. *Maybe this means something's wrong with him.* She shook her head, hard. *I'm going to drive myself crazy if I think too much.*

For the next hour Cindy busied herself cooling Champion out and making the colt comfortable in his stall. She carried in several sheaves of new straw and fluffed it up, then checked Champion's water. Finally she fed the colt a couple of plump carrots and petted him until he seemed utterly contented.

Now what? Cindy thought, slumping to the floor of the stall. She felt trapped. She couldn't take Champion out of the stall to graze, or they'd be mobbed by reporters. With her own worries about the colt, Cindy couldn't face the reporters' questioning.

"I just wish we could go home, Champion," she whispered. Cindy thought longingly of the quiet, happy days she spent with the horses at home. It would be so nice to get away from the pressures of the track, especially with Champion injured.

Cindy smiled a little, remembering the sweet, quizzical expression of Honor Bright and the way she bossed the bigger yearlings in the paddock. Then Cindy thought of Glory's Joy, born small but already strong and determined.

An image flashed into Cindy's mind of Mandy jumping Far Sailor. Cindy almost laughed as she recalled her spunky friend's wild ride over the turf jump course.

Honor, Glory's Joy, and Mandy are going to be winners,

she thought. *Honor and Joy don't let being small stand in their way. And Mandy would never let her weak legs stop her for a second.*

Cindy looked over at Champion. The colt was pushing the straw around, arranging it in new piles to his liking. "I think the real test of a winner is overcoming obstacles, boy," she said. "Everybody has problems—it's just how you deal with them."

Champion abandoned his straw game and walked over to Cindy. The colt dropped his head to look at her. His dark eyes seemed to hold a question.

Cindy reached up and hugged him. "Are you wondering if I'm going to sit here all day? No, I'm not." Cindy dug her boots into the straw and got up. "Let's take you out to graze after all," she said firmly.

Champion stepped to the door, as if he understood her words. Then he looked back to make sure she was coming.

I've never known a horse with more spirit than Champion, Cindy told herself as she led the colt out of the shed row. *Champion will do what it takes to get the job done in the Belmont—I'm sure of it.*

15

"HERE COMES THE SUPERSTAR COLT," THE ANNOUNCER called as Champion walked out onto the track for the Belmont Stakes. "Can he be the first Triple Crown winner in over a quarter of a century?"

As if in a dream, Cindy watched Champion walk out onto the track for the post parade. Nine jockeys in colorful silks and their high-strung, prancing Thoroughbreds crossed the track in front of the stands. *This is it*, she thought. *This is Champion's Triple Crown day.*

Cindy brushed back her blond hair, enjoying the warm summer day. The lush green trees at the Belmont track bent in the breeze as the field began their warm-ups. "At least we can't complain about the weather," she said.

"Don't worry." Max sounded confident. Cindy had asked her friend to watch the race with her.

"It's a perfect day for Champion." Beth patted Cindy's knee.

I sure hope so. Cindy leaned forward, watching Champion's strides closely. Champion was gliding across the track at a floating, high-stepping trot. Cindy couldn't see anything wrong with the way he was moving. But she knew the colt would have to run his absolute best to win.

Three days earlier Ashleigh had taken Champion for a long gallop. The colt had gone well, with no sign that he was favoring his injured hoof. But a leisurely gallop was much different from the blazing speed Champion would need in the race.

Champion's hoof seemed completely healed, but he was still wearing the bar shoe. That might throw off his balance and stride—not much, but enough for him to lose a world-class race like the Belmont.

"At least Sky Beauty isn't here," Cindy said to Samantha. Cindy remembered how quick the filly and her jockey had been to take advantage of every opportunity in the Florida Derby.

"Why isn't she?" Max asked.

"She's a tough competitor," Samantha said. "But her trainer has decided to run her against other fillies for now—and at distances of less than a mile and a quarter."

"He's not ruling out that Sky Beauty will start against colts again in the fall," Ian said.

Cindy was glad to hear that the game filly was doing well. But she was relieved that today

Champion didn't have to face either his worst opponent or mud. *His injury is enough for him to handle,* she thought.

Cindy felt a quick, sharp prickle of excitement as the first horse in the field, a Florida bred named Racing Trim, walked into the gate. Champion had drawn the seven position in a field of nine. *Not wonderful but not terrible, either,* Cindy reassured herself.

The field loaded quickly, the metal door clanging shut after each horse. Champion was in the six hole next to City Lady.

"Here we go," Samantha murmured. Cindy was much too nervous to speak. She stared at the track, shimmering in the heat, and waited tensely for the starting bell. The moments seemed long and heavy with promise.

The sound of the bell crashed into the silence. The crowd roared as the nine horses in the Belmont field burst from the gate.

"It's City Lady, up for the early lead," the announcer called. "Andy's Won is away in good order, running in second; Silk Stockings is third, saving ground along the rail. Back four to Wonder's Champion, off a step slow."

"What happened?" Cindy shook her head in disbelief. Champion usually broke so well from the gate! "He didn't stumble or anything, did he?"

Ian trained his binoculars on the colt. "He just broke slowly for once."

Cindy's mouth was dry. *I wonder if Champion's*

afraid, she thought, picking up her own binoculars to study the colt. *The bar shoe must be throwing off his stride. That's probably scaring him, or he just can't run as well with it. This is my worst nightmare come true!*

Cindy watched in horror as Champion fell back to fourth, then fifth as the horses rounded the clubhouse turn. "He's twelve lengths off the lead!" she gasped.

"It's a long race." Samantha gripped Cindy's shoulder. "He's not out of it yet!"

Cindy's heart was pounding, but she saw that Samantha was right. Ashleigh leaned forward over Champion's neck, and the colt responded with a bound, moving up on Andy's Won. "Yes, Champion!" Cindy breathed. As the horses had streamed into the backstretch Cindy could clearly see their positions. Champion was right behind the three frontrunners, looking for racing room.

"Wonder's Champion is asked for more run," the announcer called. "But he's got nowhere to go between horses. Andy's Won is dropping back. . . . There goes Wonder's Champion! He's through on the inside to press City Lady and Silk Stockings. City Lady is on the lead by a nose, but Wonder's Champion and Silk Stockings aren't giving up an inch!"

Ian glanced quickly at the board. "A three-way speed duel for the lead," he said. "That's not good this early in the race."

Cindy's fingers shook, rattling her program. Max reached for her hand, and Cindy smiled through

195

trembling lips. *Champion's trying so hard!* she thought. *He's just got to get by those other horses. If only he's not hurt!*

As Champion rounded the turn for home Cindy could see that the colt's mind was focused completely on running. His beautiful head held high, Champion's long legs churned deep into the loose dirt as he put away ground.

But he wasn't gaining on Silk Stockings or City Lady. The filly hung on to a half-length lead as the three frontrunners poured into the stretch. Silk Stockings was ahead of Champion by a neck.

"The bar shoe may be slowing Champion just enough so that he can't get by the frontrunners," Mike shouted.

"No, wait!" Cindy screamed. "Look!" She could hardly believe what she was seeing—in a single bound Champion had switched gears.

Champion roared onto the lead by a neck. He was into the last furlong of the race and increasing his lead with each stride!

Champion's not going to let anything stop him—not his injury, or the bar shoe, or other horses, Cindy realized. *He has so much heart—just like Wonder!*

"It's Wonder's Champion in a magnificent stretch drive!" the announcer cried. "City Lady has dropped back to second; Silk Stockings has been taken back in third position. Wonder's Champion is going for the Triple Crown! Can he do it?"

"Yes!" Cindy screamed, lunging out of her seat.

Champion was flying toward the finish. "Just a few more strides, boy, and you've got it!"

"Come on, Champion!" Max cheered.

The colt didn't disappoint Cindy or the excited, roaring crowd. Running freely five lengths ahead of Silk Stockings, Champion plunged toward the wire. He was almost there . . . he was across the finish!

"We have a Triple Crown winner!" the announcer shouted.

"You did it, boy!" Cindy cried. She fell back into her seat, overcome with emotion.

"I never saw a braver run in my life," Samantha said, sounding awed.

"This is the most incredible thing that's ever happened to Whitebrook." Mike smiled at Cindy. "Thank you so much for bringing the colt along."

"Thank him and Ashleigh!" Cindy jumped up. "Let's go tell them."

A dozen reporters were questioning Ashleigh all at once as she led the colt to the winner's circle. "We couldn't be prouder or happier on this day," she said. "I'm sure I speak for everyone at Whitebrook."

"That's for sure!" Cindy agreed. She rested her hand on the colt's sleek dark neck. "You're my hero, boy."

"Fantastic ride, Ashleigh." Mike gave Ashleigh a big hug.

"Just perfect," Cindy agreed.

The excited, happy colt snorted and lifted his head triumphantly as the officials placed the winner's blanket of carnations on his back. Cindy tried to straighten it, and Champion promptly reached around and took a bite.

"Champion, stop that!" Cindy cried, laughing. "Do you want your pictures in the history books to show you eating carnations?"

The unrepentant colt let her pull the flowers away. Then he stared straight into the cameras as he always did.

"Show-off," Mike said with a grin.

"Okay, that's it for Champion," Ashleigh finally said. She turned and gave Cindy a special smile. "Take him back, Cindy."

Smiling broadly, Cindy led the graceful, high-stepping colt toward the backside as the crowd cheered. She had to laugh as she looked at Champion. Arching his neck, the colt took little mincing steps and yanked repeatedly at the lead line. Clearly Champion knew just how well he had done and was showing off for the crowd.

"Will you consider entering him in the Dubai World Cup next year?" a reporter shouted.

Cindy stopped Champion, her eyes widening. *Wow, it would be incredible if Champion is invited to that!* she thought. The finest horses of the year were chosen to run in the Dubai World Cup, a rich new race held halfway around the world in the United Arab Emirates.

Laughing, Ashleigh held up her hand. "Next year? We'll be honored if we're invited to the Dubai World Cup, of course. But first we have to think about races this fall for our Triple Crown champion. There's the Suburban at Belmont and the Travers at Saratoga, the Jockey Club Gold Cup, and, of course, the Breeders' Cup...."

Overwhelmed with excitement, Cindy threw her arms around Champion's neck. She tightly hugged the squirming, defiant horse.

Champion stopped fidgeting for a moment and gazed intently at her. His dark eyes seemed surprised.

"I know, we've come a long way," she said. "And this is just the beginning, Champion."

The mahogany colt pranced triumphantly and tossed his head in the direction of the track. He seemed to be saying, *It's all been worth it—and I've got a lot more to give.*

JOANNA CAMPBELL was born and raised in Norwalk, Connecticut, and grew up loving horses. She eventually owned a horse of her own and took riding lessons for a number of years, specializing in jumping. She still rides when possible and has started her three-year-old granddaughter on lessons. In addition to publishing over twenty-five novels for young adults, she is the author of four adult novels. She has also sung and played piano professionally and owned an antique business. She now lives on the coast of Maine in Camden with her husband, Ian Bruce. She has two childern, Kimberly and Kenneth, and three grandchildren.

KAREN BENTLEY rode in English equitation and jumping classes as a child and in Western equitation and barrel-racing classes as a teenager. She has bred and raised Quarter Horses and, during a sojourn on the East Coast, owned a half-Thoroughbred jumper. She now owns a red roan registered Quarter Horse with some reining moves and lives in New Mexico. She has published nine novels for young adults.

THOROUGHBRED

created by Joanna Campbell

Read all the books in the Thoroughbred series and experience the thrill of riding and racing, along with Ashleigh Griffen, Samantha McLean, Cindy McLean, and their beloved horses.